THE WILL AND THE WAY

By the same Author

★

Novels

THE COLLECTIONS
THE HARNESS ROOM
MY SISTERS' KEEPER
THE LOVE-ADEPT
POOR CLARE
THE BETRAYAL
THE BRICKFIELD
FACIAL JUSTICE
THE HIRELING
A PERFECT WOMAN
THE GO-BETWEEN
MY FELLOW DEVILS
THE BOAT
EUSTACE AND HILDA
THE SIXTH HEAVEN
THE SHRIMP AND THE ANEMONE
SIMONETTA PERKINS

Short Stories

TWO FOR THE RIVER
THE WHITE WAND
THE TRAVELLING GRAVE
THE KILLING BOTTLE
NIGHT FEARS
THE COLLECTED SHORT STORIES OF L. P. HARTLEY
MRS CARTERET RECEIVES

Literary Criticism

THE NOVELIST'S RESPONSIBILITY

L. P. HARTLEY

THE WILL
AND THE WAY

HAMISH HAMILTON
LONDON

*First published in Great Britain 1973
by Hamish Hamilton Ltd
90 Great Russell Street London WC1
Copyright © 1973 by L. P. Hartley*

SBN 241 02350 5

*Printed in Great Britain
by Western Printing Services Ltd
Bristol*

CHAPTER I

As some people do after recovering from a stroke (recovery is now more common than it used to be), Mr. Handforth took on a new lease of life. He did not regard himself as immortal—since the shock of mortality had been brought so nearly home to him—but he had begun to think of life as something that was still going on and not really over. He still belonged to it: he could entertain friends, write letters, sign documents. He sometimes felt tired; but who, at 78, does not sometimes feel tired? At other times he felt quite well; he walked up and down the garden and saluted the gardener. It was quite touching how pleased the gardener seemed to be to see him. 'Why, Sir, you look twenty years younger!' 'Oh no, Hopkins,' he would say, 'but I feel better than I did.'

'We all of us think,' insisted the gardener, leaning on his spade, looking so young and healthy, and as if he spoke for cohorts of employees, 'that you look twenty years younger.'

Mr. Handforth thanked him and turned away. Why deceive oneself, or let oneself be deceived?

It happens to many people who have passed the normal span that they lose the capacity for many forms of enjoyment, and not least for friendship. Even if they still have the capacity, death has deprived them of most of their friends; and how can they make new friends when time is so short and it is too late to create the background of shared experience on which the stability of friendship depends?

Old ladies are better at making, and keeping, new friends than men are. With them, the interest, the excitement of novelty in the form of another person does not so quickly die down. Needless to say why: for them, life is a process of discovery and rediscovery in the field of human relationships, of which they never tire, whereas men tend to withdraw into themselves and look backwards to their past amorous and business achievements rather than to the present or the future, where no such prospects of personal or financial expansion lie. And sometimes, as old people will, they become critical and even turn against those who have been nearest and dearest to them.

Mr. Handforth's daughter Judith, though taken by surprise by his recovery, as everyone was, did not relax her attentions for his welfare; indeed she redoubled them, and there she made a mistake, for he, who had once been so grateful for her ministrations, with now his new sense of being his own master, began to find them irksome. Why is she always on the doorstep? he asked himself. Why is she always telling me that she and her husband are ruined? I don't believe they are, or how could they spend so much time and money coming over to see me, and telephoning me, and sending all sorts of eatables, including chocolates, which I ought not to touch?

Does she conclude I am at death's door? For I am not.

It was then that he began to think more kindly of his other daughter, Hester, who in the past he felt had been rather indifferent to his welfare. She lived on the other side of England with her husband Jack, who was a Cumberland sheep farmer, and their little boy Giles, who was six months older than Judith and Seymour's Charlotte. Except that both families had for many years spent Christmas together under Frank Handforth's hospitable roof, they seldom met each other. And then, not with hostility, but without the warmth of feeling that the tie of blood (unless it has been prematurely broken) usually inspires. Their ways lay apart and they themselves had drifted apart. Charlotte and Giles exchanged birthday letters, and gave each other Christmas presents selected by their parents; but each had only a dim

The Will and the Way

idea of what the other was like—cousin Giles, cousin Charlotte—although, as children will, they took a certain interest in each other and felt a certain curiosity about each other by virtue of their common childhood.

They did meet at other times besides Christmas, on the rare visits which Hester and Jack and Giles, coming from the distant north side of England, paid her father. Seymour, Judith and Charlotte, who lived only twelve miles away, were always asked to meet them. On such occasions there was usually a certain constraint between the grown-ups, for Hester was well aware that Judith was her father's favourite daughter. Poor, poverty-stricken Judith, whose husband had to make such an effort to make both ends meet! Could they afford to send Charlotte to a boarding-school, a good school? They doubted it. Jack was doing well, of course; there was so much more money in the North of England.

'What a nice car they have!' Judith said, when she and her father were alone together. She sighed. 'I wish we could afford one like that! Dear Daddy, I have brought you a little present—one of our chickens. I thought it might come in handy when you were having all the family to stay with you! And Charlotte has brought you something too—nothing much, only a handkerchief, but handkerchieves sometimes come in useful.'

'How kind you both are!' said her father. 'You have been so good to me, I can never repay you!' But his eyesight had not been so enfeebled by his stroke as not to notice how, at the words 'I can never repay you!' Judith's face fell.

'Darling Daddy,' she said, rising, 'Hester's here and I expect you will want to be seeing her now. I know your time is limited' (she regretted this remark as soon as it was uttered), 'and I have taken up far too much of it—I've monopolized you. You must forgive me, for I enjoy talking to you so much. But I can see Hester walking to and fro on the lawn, looking a little impatient. Shall I call her in?'

'Yes, do, my dear,' said Mr. Handforth, and during the short interval before Hester arrived his feelings, unknown to himself, had undergone a radical change.

In a way it was a relief not to have to thank anyone for anything.

Hester and her husband brought no presents, but Hester, when Judith had made way for her (they crossed each other in the doorway) said, after a moment's hesitation:

'Dear Daddy, it's good to see you looking so much better.'

'I don't think I ever looked ill,' replied her father, somewhat testily. 'I *was* ill—at least my doctor says so—and that's why this room has been made into a sort of bed-sitting room, because I'm not supposed to walk upstairs. There's the bed behind the curtain—' He pointed to the curtain with distaste. 'But we shall dine in the dining-room across the hall, like civilized people, and you and Judith—and the others—can foregather beforehand in that cubby-hole on the half-landing, which we used to call the breakfast-room. Not that we ever had breakfast there, that I remember, but it's come in handy (now that I occupy the drawing-room, which is half like a hospital ward), and I've asked Muriel to put some drinks there. I'm not supposed to have them. So I hope you won't be too uncomfortable. There's my bedroom to spare—but Judith and Seymour have annexed that.'

He stopped, a little breathless. 'First come, first served. I hope you don't mind?'

'Of course not,' Hester said. 'We shall be most happy in the South Room—as a matter of fact, it's my favourite room—and Judith and Seymour are entitled to every kind of priority—they have done so much more for you than we could ever do. Have you seen the children yet?'

'No, but I should like a peep of them before they retire.'

Hester went out into the hall.

'Charlotte! Giles!'

No answer for a minute or two, then a scurry of small feet and dark-haired Charlotte, six months younger than fair-haired Giles, burst into the room, both in diminutive pyjamas.

The Will and the Way

'We were saying our prayers,' Charlotte upbraided the assembled company—her parents, Giles' parents and their grandfather.

'We were saying our prayers,' Charlotte repeated, 'and you interrupted us!'

'Who were you praying for?' her grandfather asked.

Charlotte pursed her lips and half closed her eyes.

'That's a secret, isn't it, Giles? You are supposed to say your prayers in secret—we were told so in Sunday School.'

'Did you pray for Grandad?' her mother asked.

'We were going to, but we hadn't got up to him when you interrupted us, had we, Giles?'

'No,' said Giles nervously.

'We each have our private prayers, and we don't say them aloud, but we know who they are for. Now that you've interrupted us, we shall have to start all over again.'

She rose with a dismissive and offended air, and Giles, though much less defiantly, rose too.

'Couldn't you say your prayers down here?' asked their grandfather, rather wistfully. 'We promise not to interrupt you.'

'Oh no,' said Charlotte with decision, 'because, you see, we have to say them kneeling by our bed, and besides, we don't know where we have got up to.'

'I think you should do what your grandfather asks you to do,' said Judith, Charlotte's mother. 'He will be pleased, and God will be pleased with you for pleasing him.'

'I'm not sure I could pray with anyone looking at me,' Giles protested.

'Oh, what nonsense!' his aunt said. 'When you pray in Church everyone can look at you, and when you pray here Charlotte can look at you.'

'Oh no,' said Giles, still shocked by the idea that his orisons could be overlooked, and possibly overheard. 'You see, we say our prayers to ourselves, and bury our faces in our hands. Sometimes I hear a word of what Charlotte is saying, and she me, but we don't mean to.'

'Do you say them out loud?' asked Giles's father.

'Oh yes, Daddy, we just whisper them, otherwise they might not be heard.'

There was a pause, and the grown-ups felt rather ashamed of themselves.

'You see,' added Giles, anxious not to give offence, 'Charlotte and me, we love each other very much, and when we are together, which isn't very often, because of the distance between where we live, we decide what we shall pray for. It isn't always the same thing, because she knows different people to what I do, and wants different things to happen, but we share it out between us. Only of course there are certain people, and certain things, that we *both* pray for.'

'Dear children,' said their grandfather, his moist eyes meeting those of their respective parents, 'it's high time you went to bed. Now, if it fits in with what you want to pray for, pray for us *all*, especially for me, who have great need of your prayers.'

He suddenly looked terribly tired and old, and Judith, jumping to her feet, said, 'Charlotte and Giles, surely you can say a prayer for Grandad—it would please him so much.'

'But won't it make us late for bed?' objected Charlotte. 'You see, we have so many *other* prayers.'

'Never mind, just this once.'

The two children fell on their knees, chairless, without support, and gabbled, as though they had rehearsed it, 'Please God, take care of Grandad and make him happy for ever and ever. Amen.'

They rose to their feet with changed faces, and Charlotte said: 'May we go now? You see, Giles and I love each other.'

'Of course, darlings,' Judith said, and the four parents with their respective offspring left the room, upstairs bound, leaving Mr. Handforth in his chair.

CHAPTER II

AFTER the festivities were over, the Holroyds, father, mother and son, left for their northern home, where Jack Holroyd, with his two partners, kept a sheep farm. It was a sort of syndicate, and so far they had managed to keep on fairly good terms with each other, although farming prospects, at that time and in that part of the world, were not very rosy, and the situation of three men who are at the same time partners and competitors is never an easy one. How to divide the spoils, if there were any to divide? It needed a lot of give-and-take, to which the sons of men, being eager for the latter but not over-keen on the former, find it difficult to adjust, however sugared with *bonhomie* and drinks, and outward and indeed inward signs of reciprocity—for a partnership has to be more than a partnership in name if it is to succeed.

At the same time they had, like all businessmen, to be on their guard with each other, and when they met, even in their apparently most expansive moments—'Yes, old boy, quite right, old boy'— they each had a private reservation to keep for future use.

This moment of the year—the agricultural year—had not been a very propitious moment for any of them, and Jack Holroyd, as he drove his wife and Giles on their ten-hour journey to the northwest, was not alone in wondering, partner-wise, if he was doing the right thing and if, in his late thirties, he might not be well advised to take a new tack, and set up on his own; but as what? He had no capital to speak of, and little prospect of finding any. He did not mind unduly for himself, for he had an adventurous disposition and could greet the unknown, if not with a cheer, at any rate without alarm. But he had Hester to think of, and Giles, who must go to a preparatory school, little as his mother wanted to part with him.

These thoughts were much with him when he said to Hester, who was sitting beside him:

'I'm afraid it may be some time before we go to Middlehampstead again.'

'Oh why, Jack?'

'The expense, my dear. The journey costs quite a lot, and you have to have new clothes (I don't blame you) so as to be more or less even with Judith, and Giles is beginning to grow out of his—'

'I never said so, Daddy,' said Giles from the back seat.

'Perhaps not, but you are. And your cousin Charlotte would have noticed if you looked like a—like a scarecrow. She's very clothes-conscious, that child.'

'That's because Judith wants her to be,' said Hester. 'And what is a woman, or a girl for that matter, without clothes?'

Jack laughed.

'You should know.'

'Don't be coarse, Jack. They can afford them and we can't. They are on my father's doorstep and see him all the time. I'm devoted to my sister, but she's ambitious, and so is Seymour. They've made themselves necessary to him, especially since his stroke—I expect he helps them in heaps of ways. And Charlotte is his pin-up girl. You're fond of each other, aren't you, Giles?'

'Oh yes, Mother, we love each other. Charlotte said so too.'

'Well, I'm glad of that,' said Hester, with a touch of asperity in her voice. 'I'm very glad. You don't find Charlotte a little bossy?'

'Well, perhaps,' said ten-year-old Giles reflectively. 'But all girls are, aren't they?'

'I don't think so,' said Hester, leaping to the defence of her sex. 'I wasn't a bossy girl, was I, Jack? But of course you didn't know me at that age. I may have become bossy since.'

'Oh no, my darling,' said Jack, his eyes fixed on the wheel.

'Anyhow, *I* don't think I am,' said Hester, piqued by the charge of being overbearing. 'Have you ever found me bossy?'

'Oh no, Mother,' said Giles promptly. 'you let Daddy and me do just what we like. *Everybody* says so.'

Hester thought it would be wiser to drop the subject.

*

Giles curled up on the back seat, being no back-seat driver, and was still asleep when his parents, tired and (it must be admitted) a little cross, arrived at their farm-house in Cumberland.

'Giles!'

No answer.

'Giles!'

Still no answer.

'Is the boy dead?' asked his father fretfully.

Then Giles surfaced, rubbed his eyes, let his feet drop on to the floor of the car and said:

'I'm so sorry!'

He didn't say for what; it was a sort of universal apology.

'Never mind,' said his mother a little briskly, as if blaming him for going to sleep when they couldn't. 'We're home now.'

'Why is it dark?' asked Giles, still too sleepy to take in his whereabouts.

'Because we've been ten hours on the road,' said his mother, 'and it gets dark here sooner than it does at Grandpa's. Now be a good boy and carry Daddy's despatch case, and then he and I will bring in the rest, and then we'll have something to eat. I'm sure you must be hungry.'

'Oh, I'm never hungry,' said Giles boastfully. 'I could go for *days* without being hungry.'

'Don't be too sure,' said his father, handing him the briefcase. 'We may all be hungry before long, and then we might have to eat *you*.'

'Oh, Daddy, you wouldn't?'

'I only said "might".'

While Hester was making an omelette for their supper, Jack began to look at his correspondence, which had accumulated to an alarming extent, as correspondence will, during the short time they had been away.

Among the bills and other unwelcoming and unwelcome documents which greeted him was one from his partner, Harold Phillips:

'Dear Jack,

I don't say that things are worse since you went away on your short holiday, but they certainly are no better. I think we shall have to try to raise some cash from somewhere. I can't, and I don't think Donald can. What about trying to raise a loan from your father-in-law, whose birthday you've just been celebrating? I gather he's fairly well off. A thousand or two would make all our ends meet—for the moment at any rate. Our prospects, as you know, aren't really bad, but this credit squeeze is the devil. Do you think the old gentleman might cough up something? You told me he had a stroke and got over it, as so many people do nowadays—but still, it brings you nearer to the last lap, and if Hester or you or both of you should write and tell him we're in a rather perilous state, perhaps it might unloose his purse-strings—after all, he can't take them with him, or what's in them.

Excuse me for writing like this, but I do think we ought to take some steps, and as soon as possible.

All the best (perhaps it's too much to hope for),
    Harold.'

Jack, already tired from his journey, spent a sleepless night. He had known, more or less, that this crisis was coming, but somehow or other he had contrived to put it out of his mind. Hester had her marriage settlement, about £500 a year, that her father had settled on her at the time of their marriage. Jack had his pride and he didn't want to apply to the 'old gentleman' for further funds. But one stroke leads to another and perhaps there was not

The Will and the Way

much time to lose, and he had Hester and Giles to consider besides himself. He had no idea of how his father-in-law meant to dispose of his fortune; he did not think that Hester would be left out, but who knows? and the need was urgent. Beggars can't be choosers.

He spent the dark hours before dawn composing a letter:

'Dear Daddy,
Thank you very much for all the kindness and hospitality you showed Hester and Giles and me on your birthday party. I can't tell you how much we enjoyed it. It's only too seldom we get the chance of seeing you. It's like being in another world...

I hate to say this, but we are in rather straitened circumstances as regards the farm... and I wondered if you could find it possible to make us a small loan to tide us over? We would of course repay you as soon as we can.'

Variations of this letter went on through Jack's head all night and when morning came he still hadn't decided what to say or how to say it.

CHAPTER III

MEANWHILE, Judith Snape, Hester's sister, had not been idle, and two days after his birthday she drove over and paid her father a *visite de digestion*, as I believe the French call it.

'Darling,' she said, 'your birthday party was such fun. We did enjoy it. Everything just as it always was, and you looking so well. No, please don't get up.' Whereupon she leaned over him and kissed him fondly, before sitting down herself.

'I wish you had a birthday party every week,' she went on, 'and I hope, and so does Seymour, that you will have many, many more. Seymour of course wanted to come with me, but he's kept so busy at the office, poor fellow, that he couldn't. He only has time to snatch a sandwich.'

'But you'll stay for lunch, won't you?' her father asked.

'Well, if you press me to, Daddy, it would be rather nice, though I shall be sorry to think of Seymour bolting his sandwiches alone. I only hope it won't end in a duodenal ulcer.'

Her father looked distressed—an expression which, since his stroke, was almost endemic on his face.

'I wish he could lunch here,' he said, 'a proper lunch, I mean, not just sandwiches, which are quite filling at the time but hard on the digestion afterwards. It's only twelve miles from his office—'

'Yes, but he has to work so hard,' said Judith, 'he doesn't get more than twenty minutes off for lunch.' She sighed.

'Perhaps hard work suits him,' said her father. 'He was looking very well the other day.'

'His looks belie him,' Judith said, 'even when he's very tired, and very worried—as he happens to be now.'

'Oh dear, I'm sorry to hear that.'

'Yes, things haven't been going very well for us—at the office, I mean. And we shall soon have to be thinking about a boarding-school for Charlotte. We don't want to send her to a second-rate place. But these fees!'

'Yes, I know,' said her father, though he didn't really know.

'They're quite monstrous. I don't know what we shall do.' She stopped, and went on, inconsequently, 'I was ashamed of giving you that wretched little present of a chicken for your birthday. Farmers are so prosperous nowadays, not like us poor chartered accountants. And did you notice their clothes? Jack had a very smart suit—I love him, but he used to look so scruffy—and Giles, dear boy, was very neat and tidy—often he looks as if he had come out of a rag-bag—and as for Hester, it was quite a revelation the change that had come over her! Sometimes she looks as if she was wearing her kitchen-clothes, as I dare say I do, but really, yesterday! And that hat! I don't think it quite suited her, but it must have cost the earth! You wouldn't notice these things, but women do. I hope I don't sound envious, but I wish we could afford what they can.'

Again she suppressed a sigh.

'There is so much money in the North, at least one hears so, and farmers are especially well off.'

Mr. Handforth, who had made his money as a merchant and a company director, whatever those vague terms mean, felt that some comment was required.

'My dear Judith,' he said, 'don't think I don't appreciate all that you and Seymour have done for me. What my life would have been like after your mother died, living alone in this house, which is too big for me, rattling about like a pea in a pod, if you hadn't—'

'Don't forget, Daddy, that Seymour and I did ask you to come and live with us.'

'No, I don't forget. And Jack and Hester did the same.'

'I didn't remember that, but you couldn't have gone so far North, into that cold climate, as they must have known.'

'Well, I didn't want to be a burden on either of you. It's enough responsibility to be a parent'—he smiled—'without handing on the responsibility to one's children. So here I am—I can't tell for how long.' He smiled again. 'And I've had the joy and consolation of your constant love and friendship—and Jack and Hester's too, though they couldn't come so often, being, as you said, so far away. But—' He stopped.

'Yes, Daddy?'

'I'm sorry you and Seymour are going through a troublesome time. I hoped that the money I gave you—'

'Of course it is a tremendous help, and we are most grateful, but money doesn't go as far as it did.'

'Yes, I know, and I'm glad to know that Hester and Jack are faring so well.'

'So am I,' said Judith in a hesitant voice.

'Well, well, we must think about it,' said Mr. Handforth, and suddenly he looked very tired. 'Anyhow, it's something that you are able to stay for lunch. Just run to the kitchen, darling—I don't ring the bell more than I can help—and tell Muriel the good news.'

*

Later in the day, towards six o'clock, Mr. Handforth's old crony and contemporary, James Mackenzie, having first telephoned, paid him a visit.

'Well, old boy,' he said, 'It's very nice to see you up and about.'

'Up, yes,' said Mr. Handforth, 'but about, no—at least not much.'

'But you look a king compared to what you did,' said his friend. 'And I am sure you have heard the good news—you look as if you had, anyhow.'

'What good news?' Mr. Handforth asked. 'What good news, Jim?'

A host of expressions, astonished, puzzled, cautious, crossed his face.

'But you must have heard, Frank. I knew it was very hush-hush, but I didn't know it was as secret as all that.'

'Please tell me, Jim.'

Jim looked confounded and unhappy. He hesitated for a few moments and then said, unwillingly:

'Perhaps I ought not to.'

'Oh, come on,' said Mr. Handforth. 'If it's good news, there can't be any harm in telling me. I seem to hear nothing but bad news nowadays. Judith—' In his turn he hesitated, and a closed look came over his face.

'Yes, Judith—?' Jim asked.

Jim was Mr. Handforth's oldest friend and perhaps his only confidant. Like most people over seventy, he had lost the friends of his youth, but not the wish and the need to confide in someone.

'Yes, Judith—?' repeated Jim.

Mr. Handforth decided to come clean.

'Well, Judith lunched with me today and brought such a tale of woe.'

'Judith did?'

'Yes, she said they were in very low water, Seymour and his firm weren't getting on at all well, and what with one thing and another—sending Charlotte away to a boarding-school—they hardly knew which way to turn.'

Jim got up and began to walk about the room.

'Well, this beats me,' he said at last. 'I heard about it—not from Seymour himself, who isn't, as you know, a special friend of mine—two or three days ago, before your birthday party, and if I hadn't been bound to secrecy, I should have brought it up then, to add to the festivity of the occasion.' He went on pacing the room and knitting his brows until he looked as worried as his friend. At last he stopped his sentry-go and sat down.

'Have a drink,' said Mr. Handforth. 'They're on the sideboard. Take what you like, or what there is that suits your fancy, and would you be kind enough to give me a small gin and tonic, which is all my doctor allows me.'

He sank back in his chair. Jim poured him out a very mild gin and tonic and then, returning to the sideboard, gave himself a stiff straight whisky.

'Cheers!'

'Cheers!'

For a moment they looked at each other in silence and affection, and then Jim said, 'I really can't understand it.'

'What can't you understand?' asked Mr. Handforth, almost irritably. 'If it's good news, why not break it to me?'

'It also means breaking a promise,' Jim said, locking and unlocking his ankles, a habit he had when bothered—for the ankles appear to be seats of nervous tension.

'I can't understand why Judith didn't tell you,' Jim exclaimed. 'She must have known; how could she not have known?'

Mr. Handforth shook his head. 'You speak in riddles, Jim. *What* could she have known?'

'Well, their stroke of good luck.'

'What stroke of good luck?'

'I suppose it's a breach of confidence to tell you, but I imagined you must know. It can't be kept a secret—before long everyone will know.'

Mr. Handforth put his hands on the arms of his chair and half rose to his feet. Then he sank back again and took a sip of his drink.

'I don't think you came to give me good news,' he said. 'I think you came to tell me bad news.'

'I certainly didn't,' said Jim, giving up the struggle between what he wanted to say and what he didn't want to say. 'I came to congratulate you on Seymour's good fortune—he must have made quite a packet.'

'How, Jim?'

Jim proceeded to explain, as well as he could, the means whereby the packet had been made. There were various reasons, as

The Will and the Way

there are for many financial transactions, for keeping them secret, 'but now it seems to be all in the bag, as they say, and Seymour and Judith must be on velvet.'

After a long pause Mr. Handforth said:

'Do you suppose that Judith knew about this when she came to see me today?'

Jim shrugged his shoulders.

'How can I tell? You know your daughter better than I do.'

Jim, as her father knew, had never been very fond of Judith. Now Mr. Handforth's face was ashen as he said:

'I suppose it's possible that Seymour hadn't told Judith?'

'Quite possible,' Jim rejoined promptly. 'When you and I were young, our fathers never told their wives about their financial affairs. Women weren't supposed to know about money. I've never had a wife, so with me the question didn't arise. Perhaps Seymour didn't tell her—he's a cagey fellow, although he's your son-in-law.'

The two old gentlemen exchanged glances, but Frank Handforth did not return his friend's smile.

'How could I find out?' he asked.

'Find out what?'

'Find out if Judith knew about this scoop, or whatever they call it nowadays, when she came to see me.'

'Does it really matter?'

'It matters to me.'

'Well, I can easily find out.'

'How?'

'They don't dine until eight o'clock. I'll go round and congratulate her.'

CHAPTER IV

MR. HANDFORTH heard no more from Jim Mackenzie that evening, but the next morning he had a letter from his daughter Hester:

'Forgive me, dearest Daddy, for not writing sooner to thank you for the wonderful time you gave me on your birthday party! We don't often, in fact we never get a treat like that up here in the frozen North! But that's only by the way; the great pleasure, the great happiness, was to see you looking so much better—twenty years younger, and may you always remain so (I know this isn't physically possible!).

Judith and Seymour, I'm sure, enjoyed it all as much as we did, though Judith wasn't quite her old sparkling self. How I envy her being able to see you whenever she wants to, and whenever you want to, which must be often. She has always meant so much to you, hasn't she, your devoted daughter—as I am, and would have shown myself to be, if our paths had not lain so far apart. But that was just Fate. Jack is very busy with his sheep-farming, which is not going very well just now, but he hopes the set-back is only temporary. Farmers always complain of the weather, just as I suppose chartered accountants (for instance Seymour) sometimes complain of the Stock Market (not the stock market as we farmers understand it!).

One thing I specially enjoyed during our only too short visit was the friendship between Charlotte and Giles. I am afraid that living so far apart, they might have *grown* a little apart—she being in the midst of local social life, and us living in this wilderness where there is hardly a girl (unless you count ewes as girls) to be seen! But they seemed to be as fond of each other as ever, and Charlotte was so sweet to Giles. I think that friendship between children of that age is so touching and so genuine, especially when they seldom see each other, and have nothing to gain out of each other except love! (exclamation mark!). When I saw their two heads touching, Charlotte's so dark and Giles so fair, holding on their knees and comparing those two lovely books you had given them, and admiring, not envying, each other's, I could have cried.

You are so good to us all, dearest Daddy, entertaining us in that princely fashion, and I only wish that 250-odd miles didn't divide us, and that Jack had more opportunity to get away.

At the moment he is rather busy making up his accounts, etc. but he sends you his love, and many, many thanks for all your kindness to us. He is going to write to you in a day or two.

With all our love, dear Daddy,
Your loving
Hester.'

Mr. Handforth had just finished this letter when the telephone-bell rang. He didn't get up to answer it for since his stroke he had had an extension put beside his chair, on which, except at meal-times when guests were present, he invariably sat.

He recognized the voice.

'Hullo, Jim!'

'Hullo, Frank. I couldn't ring you up before, because Judith and Seymour were out to dinner, celebrating something—the maid didn't say what. But I went round this morning to congratulate Judith and, taken off her guard, as she sometimes is, but not often, she said:

' "Oh," she said, "the grape-vine, the bush-telegraph."

' "Oh," she said, "but I thought nobody knew."

' "Not even your father?" I said.

' "Him least of all."

' "Why?" I asked. "I thought he would have been invited to the party."

' "Oh, no," she said, "he's too old for that sort of thing, and it would excite him too much." '

'Really!' said Mr. Handforth, 'and when is this great news going to be loosed upon the world?'

'In about a fortnight, I gather, when all the odds and ends have been tied up. Meanwhile, mum's the word.'

Mr. Handforth thought for a time, and then rang up Judith and asked her to come and see him. It was about mid-day, by which time he had got over his morning dyspepsia.

'Darling Daddy,' she said, kissing him, 'how glad I am to see you!'

'I am glad to see you,' he said rather sombrely, disengaging himself from her embrace. 'At least, I think so.'

'You only think so?' she said, flabbergasted, looking as unlike the Judith he knew as he looked unlike the father she knew.

After a lifetime of unbroken continuous companionship they faced each other as strangers.

'What do you mean?' asked Judith, who was the first to recover herself.

Her father took a long time to answer.

'You came here a few days ago—I can't remember how many, my memory is so bad nowadays—and told me a hard-luck story—'

'A hard-luck story, Daddy?'

'Yes, you said that you and Seymour were in low water financially and didn't know which way to turn. You came purposely in your oldest clothes, without any make-up, to confirm the impression of someone utterly down-at-heel.'

'Oh, Daddy, you must have taken leave of your senses.'

'I may have, but since then I have recovered them, and I realize you were deceiving me. You are not hard up at at all, Judith.'

Judith lost her head.

'How do you know?'

'No matter how I know. I know that Seymour is expecting a large sum on money in the near future. Why didn't you tell me this, why didn't you tell me?'

Judith recovered herself a little, and some of its natural colour returned to her unmade-up face.

'I couldn't tell you, Daddy, not even you. I was sworn to secrecy. *No one* was to know.'

'Yet someone did know, and that someone was not your father.'

'I can guess who it was,' hissed Judith.

'No matter who it was. You have given yourself away, Judith. Even if you were sworn to secrecy, you know perfectly well that you had a large sum of money coming to you.'

Judith made a last effort to fight a rearguard action.

'Even if I did, how could I know when this large sum of money was coming to us? Sometimes these financial takeovers take *years*, and our needs were urgent. I can't understand you, Daddy, being so unlike yourself. You seem to have forgotten all that Seymour—Seymour and I—have done for you through the years, whereas Hester—'

'Don't mention her, please. And if the money was to be so long in coming, which I don't believe, which I don't believe, Judith, why did you give a party to celebrate it without even inviting me?'

'Because we know you were too ill to come.'

'I wasn't too ill to refuse. You deliberately kept me in the dark, thinking—well, I don't know what you thought.'

'We thought the same as we have always thought, Daddy,' said Judith with dignity. 'Respect, affection and *love*. Have we ever shown you anything else?'

But her father was not to be deterred.

'I think you have,' he said, 'though I wasn't aware of it until now. I think you always wanted to get money out of me, and that was the main cause of your respect, your affection and your *love*.'

'How can you say that, Father,' said Judith, leaning forward in her chair and dropping the 'Daddy', 'remembering all we have done for you? We stayed in Middlehampstead, so as to be near to you, when Seymour could have done twice as well in London, or in any large town in Yorkshire or Lancashire, where the money is. Hester and Jack went up North—they didn't care what became of you, oh no! It was left to us to hold the fort for you, and see to your wants, large and small. It hasn't been a sinecure, I can tell you, far from it. We've had to give up our holidays every now and then, when you weren't well, we've always been at your beck and call, we've *sacrificed* ourselves to you—'

Her father saw the handkerchief before it came out and was applied to her eyes. But he was unimpressed.

'You remind me of all the benefits you have conferred on me,' he said, almost breathless with agitation, 'but let me remind you of one or two things I have done for you. When you married Seymour he was good-looking, I admit that, but quite penniless, and it was I who set him up in business in Middlehampstead; there was plenty of competition then, and he wouldn't have found a foothold but for me. How would you have liked it, Judith, to sink from job to job, here in England or perhaps abroad, with no other asset but a good-looking husband, who might soon have got tired of you? Don't suppose I don't know what he is like—'

'Father, what do you mean?'

'You know quite well what I mean. He knew that I had a liking for him, just as I have for you, and between you, you decided to make yourselves necessary to me—oh, don't imagine I wasn't grateful to you for all you did, and I've shown my gratitude in more ways than you know of.'

Drying her eyes, Judith shot him an interrogative glance.

But her father swept on.

'But now I know you both for what you are—schemers. You wanted to drain the well dry—it is nearly dry, but not quite.'

The effort to relieve his feelings, which were of such recent date, not more than a few days old, suddenly brought a revulsion, and looking at Judith, he saw her as she had been as a child, a girl, as a young woman, as a bride (not a happy moment for him), advancing to maturity, as a mother, the mother of Charlotte, a devoted mother, but not less devoted to him, still his prop and stay, his staff of life, until when?—until the few days ago which had changed the whole picture and made nonsense of it.

Earth knows no hell like love to hatred turned, and in the short time that remained to them before Judith, weeping, was for a moment unable to find the door into the hall, Mr. Handforth thought of her simply as a designing woman, who had spent her life sucking his vital juices, especially his monetary juices (thank goodness he still had some wherewithal left), in the effort to get more and more and more.

When she came to him with her hard-luck story she was probably better off, or had an immediate prospect of being better off, than he was or had ever been.

She was like a good meal that suddenly turns sour on the stomach; and he wished he had never begotten her. Every kindness she had ever done him now seemed to have had an ulterior motive—she was trying to get something out of him—and especially hateful to his mental eye was the garb of affection she had put on whenever she came near him. The kindnesses she had shown him, the trouble she had taken over him, were so many more examples of her blood-sucking hypocrisy. She was a vampire, had always been a vampire.

Sitting alone, unstirring, he saw his face in the looking-glass opposite. How pale he was, or if not how pale, how unlike the image his imaginary self-portraits had created for himself! So different, so wild, so staring, so glaring, so unfriendly, so hostile—no, so utterly unresponsive—to anything he saw. He was frightened; anger was working in him; from his head to his toes he could feel it at work, transforming him from someone he had been to someone he was not, but who he soon would be.

CHAPTER V

Two days later he got a letter from Cumberland:

'Dear Daddy,

I can't tell you how grateful Hester and I are for the cheque. Please forgive me for not writing sooner to thank you for an absolutely smashing birthday party. We live in the hope that you will see many more birthdays.

Giles loves the book you gave him and he simply worships the model sailing-ship, and he takes it to bed with him every night, and he puts it on a sort of stool he has borrowed for the purpose, so that he can look at it every time he wakes up.

We all look forward to our next visit to Middlehampstead to see you.

Thank you again for your very generous cheque, which came at a very opportune moment.

With much love from us all,
Jack.'

*

'Dear Giles,

Thank you very much for your letter, in spite of the spelling mistakes, they are very hot about that in my school which is very expensive, but I daresay they aren't so keen about it at yours.

We had a very large banquet a few nights ago to celebrate a merger, if you know what that means, that Dad had arranged between two companies and it seems that I shall be able to go to the best dancing-class in the town. I don't suppose you have a dancing class where you are; it's so far from anywhere, and I know you don't like dancing, but if you could learn it even a little we could have grate fun the next time you come down here, because there are no boys I like as much as you, even if they can dance and you can't.

Dad and Mum are making all sorts of plans for the future. I don't know what they are, and I mustn't tell you even if I did, because it is so secret, but we may be moving away from this house, which is rather small for us, although it's not so small as yours, when Grandad dies and we don't have to be near him.

I shall like to see your boat, even if it does fall over on its side, specially if Grandad gives you another, and I want you to see my pony, which is a peach to look at but not very good-tempered. Mum wants Grandad to give me another instead.

I wish you weren't so far away. There are plenty of boys here, of course, and I don't suppose there are many girls your way, but I shall always be,

Your loving and affectionate cousin,
Charlotte
X X X X X X X X'

Hester looked round the kitchen, which seemed empty, except for its pile of unwashed plates, since Giles had been sent off to bed.

'He was pleased with his letter from Charlotte, wasn't he? Perhaps he's put it under his pillow. When I was a lad like him, I used to put all sorts of things—letters and other things—under my pillow. I suppose I thought they were guardian angels.'

'But do you need them now?'

'No, because I have you.'

CHAPTER VI

MR. HANDFORTH in his old age, in his second childhood—advanced by his stroke—had kept his wits about him, and they, as old people's wits sometimes will, inclined him to be critical of those who were nearest and dearest to him.

Undoubtedly, it was Judith who was—or who had been—nearest and dearest to him. Throughout the many years of his widowerhood—how many!—she had been at his beck and call, neglecting, as she herself had said and as he had had ample opportunities of confirming, her own family and her own affairs to console him in his solitude. She had even suggested, and he had gratefully though guiltily agreed to her suggestion, that her family would have been larger than it was, that Charlotte might have had brothers and sisters, as Seymour hoped she would have, if she had not felt that her father was her first priority.

This combined feeling of guilt and gratitude he had tried to acknowledge to her from time to time, by presents smaller and greater; and he had made and re-made his Will many times, with the object of leaving the residue of his estate, already much reduced by Judith's inroads on it, in unequal shares, to Judith and Hester—shares that should seem equal, though they were not. Thus he got his house and its contents valued at a very low figure, well knowing that it would be worth far more at his death, to balance a rather higher figure of shares to Hester, the value of which he had good reason for thinking would go down rather than up.

Not that he was not fond of Hester, but in his mind and

affections she had always played second fiddle to her sister; though younger, she had married earlier; like an almost unfledged bird she had abandoned the nest, and made another for herself far, far away. It was natural, of course; Jack had swept her off her feet, she had thrown in her lot with him, leaving her father to Judith's very tender mercies.

How can one feel towards someone who, for the most natural reasons in the world, has thrown one over as one feels towards someone who, for the best reasons in the world, has stayed by one's side?

But were they the best reasons in the world? No, Mr. Handforth decided, they were the worst; everything his daughter Judith had done for him, all her kindness and her assiduous attentions when he had been alone and/or ill, had been inspired by one motive, and only one: the greed of gain. At last she had shown herself in her true colours—the colours, whatever they were, of a vampire.

How innocent by comparison had been Hester's and Jack's thank-you letters for his birthday party hospitality!

All night long Mr. Handforth brooded over these anomalies, until the name of Judith became anathema to him and Hester only evoked the Evening Star.

Tossing to and fro in his bed, he knew that his mind was failing him, his judgement was failing him, and probably his life was failing him. But despite these rational convictions, a deep-seated instinct urged him to redress the balance, the balance between him and his two daughters, one of whom had been so self-seeking and the other so self-effacing. Well, before it was too late he would not be the fool King Lear had been; with no other fool but himself to remind him of his folly, the past had been obliterated, and what did the future hold? On whom, or on what, could he rebuild the ruins of his life on a safer foundation? For he was not a man who gave way to despair.

In the morning, while his resolution still held, he rang up his old friend, the Reverend Frederick Morris.

'Fred, will you do me a kindness?'

'Any time, Frank.'

'Could you come along here now, just for a moment?'

Mr. Handforth explained why.

'Of course—I'll come at once.'

'I've asked James Mackenzie to come round too.'

When the Rev. Morris arrived, James Mackenzie was already there and Mr. Handforth was in bed, not looking too well.

'You must excuse me,' he said, 'but it is rather urgent. It's my new Will.'

'And you want us to witness it?' asked James Mackenzie.

'If you will be so kind.'

'And do you want us to read it?'

'I think it would be better if you did.'

The two men scanned the document and turned to each other.

'It will make a considerable difference to some people,' said James.

'I know it will. That's why I asked you to come, and for the pleasure of seeing you both. Seymour will certainly be a rich man, if he isn't already, and I don't want him to be any richer than he is, or will be.'

When the proceedings were over and the new Will duly dated and signed and witnessed, and they had drunk each other's health in a rather funereal fashion, Fred said:

'It must have been a bit of a strain, all this. If I were you I should take a rest now. And I think you should ask your solicitors, Watkins and Harborough, to come along and destroy this—' He tapped the old Will which was lying on the bed. 'Then all will be in order.' But as he and James were leaving the bedroom, he turned and said, 'Remember, Frank, you're acting on impulse. One cannot foresee what one's reactions will be in a month's, or a week's, or a few hours' time. You may want to cancel this Will you've just made. And if so, don't hesitate to let us know, we're always at your beck and call.'

Mr. Handforth sat up in bed, the new Will on his right hand

and the old Will on his left. He glanced from one to the other, and sometimes he could hardly distinguish between them, so confused was his mind. To add to his confusion were his friend's parting words, which hinted that he might want to change his mind. 'Never, never,' he thought, 'I would rather die!'

Shakily he rose to his feet and, scarcely aware of what he was doing, went to his library, the new Will in his hand. Looking vaguely at the bookshelves, he suddenly remembered the advice of an old friend, who had a horror of burglars, that the best place to hide money—money in the form of notes—was between the pages of a book. 'They will never look there,' she said. The new Will represented money, and he had got it into his head that someone might see it, and even steal it, before he died. But where? The higher the better—the higher the fewer (an old tag came into his mind)—and he stretched upwards as far as he could reach, took out the middle volume of Gibbon's *Decline and Fall*, and having inserted the Will in the middle, stepped back. But where were his feet? Where were his legs? They didn't support him; they didn't belong to him; they didn't belong to himself. The thud of his fall was the last sensation he had. He had no time to remember, if he had been in a state to remember, that his first Will was lying open on the dining-room table.

CHAPTER VII

AFTER Mr. Handforth's death, a thorough search was made by the solicitors, Messrs. Watkins & Harborough, but the only document found was his Will dated three years before. It was at last agreed, and decided, that Mr. Handforth had relented and destroyed the Will he had made so suddenly, shortly before his final stroke, and that the previous Will, found lying on the dining-room table, revealed quite obviously his last wishes.

His funeral was attended by a large muster of people, including of course his two daughters and their husbands, and Charlotte and Giles. Judith, it was observed, was in half-mourning, while Hester was in deepest black; the sons-in-law wore their darkest suits and their most formal and funereal expressions. Charlotte was becomingly arrayed in a dress that combined mourning with fashion; Giles, with a thin black tie round his thin neck and wearing trousers for the first time, as his mother did not think that shorts were suitable for a funeral, kept studying his hidden knees and feeling the strangeness round them.

Everyone knows what a funeral is like, and few people want to be reminded of it. Judith kept a straight face, which was like a death-mask of her own; Hester, in tears, had frequent recourse to her handkerchief; the brothers-in-law, really so unlike each other —Jack tall, fair, loose-limbed and bucolic, Seymour dark, spare, short and obviously town-bred—seemed to have a common facial resemblance in the brotherhood of death.

They all walked up the aisle together and took their places in the front pew; only Charlotte was impressed by the honour of this position. Giles, in his unaccustomed trousers, was bewildered and could not connect the ceremony with anything in his daily life. He felt the awe of the solemnity of the occasion, seeing it reflected in the faces of the mourners round him, at which, when not burying his face in his hands, he every now and then took surreptitious glances. But the fact of death, as something that would ultimately happen to him, meant nothing to him; and what he was physically most aware of was his trousers rubbing against his knees, and mentally he kept asking himself, 'Shall I be allowed to wear them afterwards?'

When the service was over, some of the mourners followed the coffin to the graveside. Giles, not from any wish to be in at the death, but from a desire for conformity and a desire not to be left out, would have liked to follow the cortège; and he would be able to boast to his school-friends, most of whom were funeral-free, that he had looked down into a grave, but his mother whispered to him, on the church steps, 'There is a car' (she pointed to it) 'to take you and Charlotte back to the house. Wait for us there, we shan't be long.'

For part of the short journey Charlotte wept, dabbing her eyes with an embroidered handkerchief and closing them between sobs, much as her mother had; then she said:

'You aren't crying, Giles. You ought to.'

'I know,' said Giles, 'but boys don't cry so easily as girls. For one thing, we're not supposed to; and for another, I didn't know Grandad half as well as you did. I would cry if I could,' he added, wistfully.

'Could you cry if I died?' Charlotte asked.

Giles tried to consider this. He could not imagine Charlotte dying, any more than he could imagine dying himself.

'I suppose I could,' he said, 'if it was a very, very long way off.'

'Do you love me very much?'

'Oh yes, of course,' said Giles promptly, relieved at being asked such an easy question. 'I love you very much, more than anyone except perhaps Mummy and Daddy, and I love them because they love me.'

Charlotte seemed only half satisfied with this answer.

'Don't you think I love you?'

Giles was man enough to be afraid of the word 'love'.

'Yes, I'm sure you do,' he answered evasively, looking out of the window, and away from Charlotte. 'But it's different for a girl.'

'Why is it different?'

Giles's schoolboy contemporaries thought it was 'soppy' to be in love with girls. He couldn't explain this to Charlotte, so he said hastily, trying but unable to avoid the dreaded word, 'I think girls love more than boys do.'

'I don't believe you love me,' said Charlotte. Out came her handkerchief again, and the tears she had shed for Grandad Handforth were now shed for herself.

Giles, as an older person might have been, was stricken with guilt and remorse.

'Of course I love you,' he protested, and turned and in a fumbling groping way, for he was no expert at kissing, tried to dry the tears from off her watery face.

At this moment the car drew up at the door of Mr. Handforth's one-time residence and the driver, looking sad for both of them, for he had children of his own, and perhaps wishing that these were old enough to give him a tip, helped them out. The front door was open and in they went.

*

The house had the atmosphere of most houses in such circumstances—blinds flapping, air blowing through and above all, a sense of emptiness.

This was more apparent to Charlotte, who knew the house so well, than it was to her cousin Giles, whose visits had been so infrequent. But even she did not know which way to go; the downstairs rooms were so drained and changed.

The Will and the Way 33

'This way, Miss Charlotte,' said the maid, perceiving her hesitation, and led them both into the dining-room where, on the sideboard and on sundry small tables ranged about, were the funeral bake-meats and a plentiful array of bottles and glasses.

Neither Charlotte nor Giles had ever been to a cocktail party, so they did not realize that this was an ironic travesty of one. But they were both hungry and thirsty, as children mostly are, and they looked with greedy eyes at the delicacies spread around and the empty plates waiting to receive them.

To their sensitive nostrils the smell of food, denied them from much earlier in the day, became almost unbearable.

'Do you think?' asked Charlotte, with her eyes on an inviting canapé.

But Giles had scruples.

'Oughtn't we to wait for the clergyman to say Grace? Grandad always said Grace.'

'I don't think he would now at such a time as this,' said Charlotte doubtfully. 'I mean,' she corrected herself, 'the clergyman wouldn't. It isn't like an ordinary meal, is it? There are no places for one thing and only those few chairs scattered about, and they would be for old people like Mummy and Daddy—and,' she added as an afterthought, 'your Mummy and Daddy. Besides, no one need know that we've eaten anything, if you can remember to stop munching when they come in. It's easy to tell if you're eating anything because you make a noise like this—' and Charlotte, with working jaws, made a parody of Giles chewing his food. 'I know you can't help it,' she added, noting his hurt look, 'and we were both told to bite each mouthful thirty-two times, like Mr. Gladstone. But you needn't *show* you're biting it.' And in pantomime she demonstrated how to chew without the maxillary convulsions being apparent. 'Now it would be different if we drank anything,' she went on, with a longing look towards the glasses, 'because then they'd be bound to see, and it isn't nice to drink out of somebody else's glass anyhow. I don't see why, but that's what grown-ups think. Now I'll give you this,' she said, at the cost of some self-sacrifice putting her favoured canapé into Giles' reluctant hand, 'and I'll get a sandwich from the table over there, and no one will be any the wiser.'

Suiting the action to the word, she darted across the room, leaving Giles to digest, literally and metaphorically, the sensations of Adam after he had been tempted by Eve.

Returning to his side, she said with a loving look, 'I know I ought not to speak with my mouth full, but you will marry me sometime, won't you, Giles?'

'Of course I will,' he said, as distinctly as the powdery, crumbly canapé, which obstinately resisted being swallowed, allowed him to. 'Any time you like,' he added, as boldly as any bridegroom.

'Then kiss me.'

Much as he disliked this effeminate and derided practice, he kissed his cousin for the second time that day. They they sprang apart, as older and more guilty lovers might have, for there was a shuffling of feet and a murmur of voices outside the open doorway, and the mourners from the graveside straggled in, glancing at each other with looks that forbade smiles, but turned more readily to the tempting display of eatables and drinks on the sidetables. As Charlotte had foretold, the clergyman who had taken the service did not say Grace; but later on he showed his gratitude in a more material manner, by eating heartily.

Meanwhile Judith caught up Charlotte in her arms and Hester embraced Giles. 'Darlings,' they said, each in her own way, 'you must be *famished*!' and quickly led their offspring to the sidetables where plenty reigned.

Charlotte and Giles took full advantage of this invitation to gourmandize: Giles, indeed, forgot his cousin's injunction not to chew too obviously and received from her an admonitory glance.

The combined, but essentially irreconcilable, sadness and relief of the occasion was lost on them; the breeze blowing through the empty hollow rooms, as though to exorcize the soul of its departed owner, the shadows from the flapping blinds—a strange mixture of light and dark, where no such mixture had ever been before. The elders responded to this, each in his or her own way; never a happy way, though solaced by food and wine.

Only Charlotte and Giles felt it to be a party, and were sorry when their fathers and mothers, with more than one backward glance into the interior whose occupant they had known so well, and who was still, even in death, so much a part of themselves, gave their fellow mourners an interrogative look, and led the way out.

CHAPTER VIII

WHEN Mr. Handforth's Will was proved it was found that his estate was larger than it had been thought to be, and that more than three-quarters of it, four-fifths in fact, had been left to his elder daughter Judith, 'in recognition of and gratitude for the fact that during the long period of widowerhood she had spared no pains to make his life as comfortable and happy as possible, at whatever cost to her own convenience.' 'I owe her more than I can say,' he wrote.

'I don't think we need tell him, do you, Jack?'

'Tell who what?'

'Tell Giles about Grandad's Will.'

Jack grunted.

'No, what good will it do? He'll find out soon enough. He's too young to know how it affects him. We could have sent him to a public school—we can't now. But does it matter? I never went to one myself, and some of those public schools are dens of vice from what I hear. Giles isn't a strong character, and I dare say he'll be better off at the local grammar school, if it hasn't been abolished, where we know the Headmaster can keep an eye on the boy.'

Hester, who had also cherished loftier ambitions for Giles, gave a sigh.

'Can you go to University from a grammar school?'

'Of course you can, idiot. Mr. Thirkenwacke is a live wire and doesn't let the grass grow under his feet. And as things are today, Giles will be none the worse off for being a poor man's son, no hee-haw and that sort of business.'

The Will and the Way

Hester considered this.

'He's in bed asleep now,' she said, looking at the electric clock which showed half-past seven. 'At least I hope he's asleep—he's said his prayers. He always prays for Charlotte, little as she needs it. "Please, God, take care of Charlotte." I should have thought Charlotte could well take care of herself.'

'Don't be bitter, Hester,' Jack said, 'it isn't like you, and I dare say we all need someone's prayers.'

'You're too tolerant,' snapped Hester, 'you're too easy-going—if you weren't, we shouldn't find ourselves in the state we are in now. If we had sucked up to Daddy as my sister Judith did, we should be in Easy Street. I know she was closer to him, in every sense of the word, than we were, and you, Jack, never tried to bridge the distance—you were too proud, or too lazy, or too indifferent—but the result was that Judith got everything her own way.'

Jack rose and walked about the kitchen, which his fair head, and his broad slender shoulders and his commanding height, seemed to fill.

'Don't let's worry about it, Hester,' he said, placatingly, 'we can't do anything about it now.'

'No, perhaps not,' retorted Hester, 'in spite of that rumour that Daddy made another Will. But why do you think he left four-fifths of what he died possessed of to Judith and Seymour, and only one-fifth to us?'

'I don't think he meant to deal unfairly with us,' Jack said. 'He couldn't have guessed that his house, being in the middle of the town, with the garden round it, would turn out to be worth so much. I happen to know that it was originally valued at half as much as Seymour and Judith eventually sold it for. And the shares, well, they went down. Anybody's shares can go down. Seymour had to pay capital gains tax on Middlehampstead, don't forget that.'

'Yes, but they somehow wangled it with the Tax Inspector, who is a chum of Seymour's.'

'That may be.'

'But the net result,' said Hester, 'is that they are well off and we are badly off. We aren't paupers, Jack, but we are sinking in the social scale. Giles won't be a farm-labourer, but he won't be much above it, whereas Charlotte, with all that money coming to her, may be a Countess.'

She lowered her voice.

'And did you know something?'

'What?'

'Well, just before Grandad died, Judith went to him and said they were terribly hard up, they couldn't afford the money for Charlotte's schooling, and all the time she knew about this merger, which doubled, which *doubled*, their capital.'

'I did hear something about it,' said Jack, shortly. 'I don't know how true it was.' He looked round the ample kitchen, in which the pots and pans were kept bright and shining by Hester's indefatigable hands, but which, as far as the walls and the paint and the creaking cupboards went, sadly needed doing up.

'Never mind, old girl,' he said, putting his long arm across her shoulders, a gesture of endearment to which she never failed to respond, 'somehow or other we shall make both ends meet.'

Hester busied herself with preparing their supper, the smell and flavour of which appealed to Jack's nostrils and through them to his appetite, whetted by the physical toils of the day, up and down the fells. Coming from a lower stratum of society than she did, notwithstanding his *bon animal* appeal, which was at its best in the kitchen, he was readier to accept the dictates of Fate.

But Hester, as she put his heaped-up plate before him, an emblem of love which had gained force and sweetness for her on its way from the oven, couldn't resist returning to the old subject, couldn't resist thinking of Judith and Seymour in their diningroom, their dinner prepared by a cook.

As Jack fell to hungrily without waiting for Hester to begin, she said, as she laid her plate on the table:

'Don't you think it's rather odd, Jack?'

'What's odd?' he asked, between large mouthfuls.

The Will and the Way

'It's odd about Daddy's Will. I know that Judith did much more for him than I was able to do, but all the same—'

'Don't bother about it,' said Jack, intent on his food.

'But I do. I don't think it was fair. Just because Judith—'

'Why,' said Jack, raising his flaxen eyebrows, 'would you rather have Seymour than me?'

It didn't take Hester long to decide between them.

'No, but I don't think you understand, Jack. We could, we ought to be quite well off, whereas you have to slave away in your shirt-sleeves—'

Jack took a hasty look at his muscular, sunburnt arms and turned his shirt-sleeves down.

'It isn't really fair. I grant that Judith has given us Grandad's library, because she never reads a book, but where shall we put it?'

'Oh, anywhere,' said Jack. 'Ther're heaps of places. The old granary, for instance.'

'Yes, perhaps, if it isn't damp. And then Charlotte—Giles is fond of her, I know he is, but she'll turn up her nose at coming here.'

'Oh,' said Jack, swilling round his plate with a piece of bread, 'you always look on the dark side, Hester. Charlotte will forget all about Giles, you may be bound, and find another boy, or boys, more within her income-bracket.'

Hester agreed to this, verbally, although in her mind she didn't accept it: her niece meant more to her than any other girl within her sister's income-bracket.

Meanwhile, it was gratifying to see Jack's empty plate, and his face bright with the pleasure of being with her.

'Of course Charlotte would be a good catch if Giles could land her,' said Jack, reflectively.

'What disgusting expressions you use.'

'Well, the poor lad won't get much from us, and I don't see him making his living as a farmer. Giles has no head for business, and would never get the better of the farmers round about.'

Pursuing his own train of thought, he said:

'Seymour must be pretty warm by now.'

'Pretty, no,' said Hester promptly, 'and as for warm, what do you mean by warm?'

'Just well off.'

'How unpleasant. Literally, he's as warm as a refrigerator. And he's managed to chill Judith, too. When she was a girl—she's older than I am, as you know—she was often great fun, a bit spiky, which was why she didn't marry sooner than she did. Men were afraid of her. But Seymour wasn't: he isn't afraid of anyone, or anything, except losing money. And he's put an icicle into Judith's heart—'

'What makes you think so? She seems to me quite an ordinary girl, a bit avaricious and ambitious, but so are lots of women.'

Hester disregarded this.

'You're very simple in some ways, Jack.'

Jack bridled, and lit a cigarette.

'I don't think I'm any more simple than the next man.'

'Yes, you are. You didn't notice, for instance, that when you and I and Giles went down for Daddy's birthday we put on new clothes for the celebration—and they cost quite a lot—whereas Judith and Seymour and Charlotte wore clothes that might have come out of a jumble-sale.'

'And what do you infer from that?'

'That they wanted to impress him with how hard up they were. And yet they knew, or Seymour knew, that they were bringing off this merger, which has been worth thousands of pounds to them.'

'Good luck to them,' said Jack.

'Well, I don't know. I was very fond of Daddy, and so was he of me, I think—he used to call me his little darling. But I left home when I was eighteen, to come here—which I've never regretted, Jack, I've never regretted—and Judith and Seymour were on his doorstep and did more for him, in his long widowhood, than we could ever have done.'

'You've said that before,' said Jack, 'but what difference does it make?'

The Will and the Way

'Don't you see,' said Hester, exasperated, 'that it makes *all* the difference? Judith's marriage-settlement was larger than mine, not only because he was better off, or "warmer" as you say, when she married than when I did, but also because she had three years in which to make herself necessary to him—and she did. We couldn't afford to have a child for three to four years—they had one at once, which is why Giles and Charlotte are much the same age. *They* could have had more children in their refrigerator if they'd wanted to; we couldn't.'

'Well, things turn out like that,' said Jack, gently puffing his cigarette, 'and I hope you don't regret it, because I don't.'

'I do regret it,' exploded Hester, indignantly, 'and what's more I resent it, for your sake, and for mine, and for Giles's. Why should we have to live counting every penny, while they live in affluence? And there's another thing—'

'Yes?' said Jack, lighting another cigarette.

'I wonder if Daddy knew when he made his Will that Seymour and Judith were coming in for this large sum of money?'

'He couldn't have done,' said Jack. 'It was made more than three years ago, before your father had his stroke, and there was no question of the merger then.'

Hester looked almost disappointed.

'But all the same,' she said, defending herself, 'he must have known that his house, with its four acres of garden in the middle of Middlehampstead, would be worth a lot of money—even if it was undervalued for probate—and he left it to Judith.'

'Yes, but the District Valuer quickly stepped in and revalued it, and Seymour couldn't fix that,' grinned Jack.

Hester smiled softly.

'It's too late to bother about it any more,' said Jack. 'The Will's the Will, and we can't do anything about it. I liked your Dad,' he added inconsequently, 'He was always very nice to me, and I wasn't much of a catch, was I? Just a poor chap, with a dim future, sheep-farming. And yet he seemed to like me.'

He caught sight of his reflection in the looking-glass opposite.

He wasn't vain of his appearance, and it still flatters me, he thought.

There was another looking-glass, a wedding-present, in which Hester could also see his reduplicated face.

'I'm not blaming you, darling,' she said. 'How could I? I'm not blaming anyone, though I think Judith and Seymour did perhaps take a little advantage of their nearness to Daddy.'

'Do you think he could have made another Will?'

Jack hesitated. He had heard a rumour, a vague, stifled rumour, that his father-in-law, on his death-bed, had made a second Will. But this Will, if it existed, had never been found, and there was no likelihood it ever would be.

'Don't think about it,' he said, and stretched out his big hand to meet his wife's across the table. 'I'm happy as I am, Will or no Will.'

Hester held his hand, with all its mounds and crevices of manual toil, for a moment, and then said:

'It was Giles I was really thinking of. You said he would be sure to find out about Daddy's Will sometime. Wouldn't it be better to tell him *now*, before he realizes how much better off Charlotte is than he is, than let him wait to find out for himself?'

'I doubt if he knows much about money,' Jack said. 'He takes after me in that. I should let him find out for himself—if he does find out. Boys of his age aren't money-conscious—they're thinking of all sorts of other things.'

'But Charlotte?' asked Hester, relinquishing Jack's wrist, which was still stretched like an advanced post in battle across the tablecloth.

'Oh, let's forget about Charlotte,' Jack said.

CHAPTER IX

TIME passed and Giles went to a Secondary Modern School in the neighbourhood, where he was quite happy, for he was a born conformist, and wanted to be like the other boys of his age, not cleverer or less clever, not better at games or less good, not winning extra marks for good conduct, or losing them for bad conduct, in fact an unexceptionable example of what a schoolboy of his time ought to be.

'Giles is doing very well,' his father said. 'He's just like all the others. I'm glad I didn't have the money to send him to one of those posh schools we once thought of. There, he might have stuck out like a sore thumb. Here, he's got all the others to keep him company—he works like they do, he feels like they do, and even *looks* like they do! When I collect him from the bus, I'm never sure which of them he is.'

Hester hesitated for a moment. 'I've noticed the same thing,' she said. 'He's accepted uniformity with a will. They ought to be dressed alike, oughtn't they?'

'Well, they are. Haven't you noticed it? Grey shorts, blue blazers with the school crest embroidered on the left breast, a lion couchant-passant-regardant—I can never remember which—and a blue cap with the same sort of lion on it.'

'I don't see Giles as a lion,' said his mother. 'He doesn't want to devour anybody. A sheep would be more suitable to him, and more in keeping with us.'

'I don't think a sheep is an heraldic animal,' argued Jack.

'It is in the Law Courts.'

'The Law Courts! The last place I'd expect to see a sheep.'

'Yes, I see what you mean; but it is the arms of the Middle Temple, but whether it's a true symbol—'

Jack laughed. 'I hope not. But I don't know much about heraldry—why should I?—and I've never *seen* a sheep on a crest or coat of arms.'

'But you have read the Bible?' said Hester.

'I did as a boy,' said Jack, 'and I see what you mean. But do you also mean that you would rather Giles was a sheep than a lion?'

'I can't answer that,' said Hester, looking at his tawny countenance and predatory yellow eyes, with their glint of green. 'You are a shepherd of a superior kind, even if you look more like a lion. But what I wanted—what we both wanted—for Giles was that he should be able to choose between the two. Now he's definitely a sheep.'

Jack stripped off his jacket with its frayed cuffs, for the room was warm, and the divesting himself exuded an atmosphere of sweat and masculinity that he was unaware of, though his wife was not.

'Still harping on the old grievance?' he said, giving her a leonine look.

'Yes, I am,' said Hester, 'and I believe that if you had belonged to my family you would have felt the same. Why should Judith and Seymour have had so much more than we had? In addition to what they were already going to have, as Daddy must have known.'

'How could he have known?'

'Never mind how—I think he *did* know.'

'Well, whatever he left us, helped us to turn the corner—we were nearly on the rocks, and now we aren't.'

'If Daddy had left us fair shares, not only should we have been more comfortably off, but we could have sent Giles to a school where he could have chosen between being a lion and a sheep.'

'I think he will be happier as a sheep,' his father said. 'Who wouldn't be?'

'How can you say that?' cried Hester, inflamed. 'You may

The Will and the Way

pretend to be a sheep, but you are a lion in sheep's clothing—not a wolf,' she added, 'I almost wish you were.'

She sighed deeply.

'And now there's this invitation,' she said.

'What invitation?'

'This invitation to Charlotte's birthday-party—she's sixteen—she's six months younger than Giles.'

'And you don't want to go?'

'Of course I don't want to go, to meet all those smart friends of Judith's, none of whom I know.'

'Was it you alone who were asked?'

'Oh no, we were all three asked.'

'Why don't you say we can't go? You could say it's the lambing season—it isn't, of course, but they wouldn't know.'

'I can't say that,' said Hester petulantly. 'Judith would see through it in a moment. No, but I should have to get a new outfit. It would cost us *pounds*.' Her voice dropped at the word.

'I don't see why,' said Jack, leaning his elbows on the table and pining for lunch. 'I don't see why we should go if we don't want to. And if we do, you still have your best black dress, and I have my one good suit, which is a bit old but not too bad—'

Hester looked at her husband pityingly. 'But my dress is out of date.'

'But isn't black always fashionable for women? Don't they always look well in it?' And he harrowed her with the stare of his amber eyes.

'Nonsense,' she said, resisting it. 'You're right about black—but black yesterday isn't the same as black today. I suppose your suit is all right, but Giles—'

'Yes?'

'He's outgrown everything.'

'Why should we bother to go?' asked Jack, feeling hungrier and hungrier. 'Why don't you say that we are haymaking and can't spare the time?'

Hester didn't answer at once.

'Well,' she said at length, 'Judith is my sister after all, and blood is thicker than water.'

'Could we have a drink?' asked Jack. 'I've been out all the morning chasing those damned sheep, while Seymour has been sitting on his backside in the office, telling his secretary to answer his letters and arrange for mergers.'

'There's a little gin left,' said Hester, and he lapped it up.

Encouraged by this, he said:

'You say it will cost us pounds to be fit to be seen, and we shan't know anyone, so what is the point of it?'

'I must go and look at the cooker,' said Hester. Returning she said, 'I think Judith *wants* us to go. After all, she is my sister.'

'I thought you said you hadn't any clothes,' said Jack. 'I can wear my smock of course, if you think it would be suitable.'

Hester ignored this.

'And there's another reason. Charlotte particularly wants to see Giles.'

'Why?'

'She's always been attached to him, in the way that cousins sometimes are.'

'I don't believe in these boy-and-girl friendships,' said Jack, sniffing hungrily at the smell of oncoming lunch. 'And if she wanted to see him so much, why couldn't she have come here? We could have provided her with plenty of mutton.'

'Yes, but it's different in her case. Don't you see,' Hester added, 'That when a girl in her situation, with plenty of money and plenty of young men to choose from, *specially* want to see Giles, it would be a pity to thwart her? There may be nothing in it, of course, and I don't know how Giles feels—he hasn't seen Charlotte for I don't know how long—but I think it's time we all got together.'

'Clothes included?' said Jack.

'Yes, clothes included. We may be poor relations, but we *are* relations, and as Charlotte made such a point of wanting to see Giles—'

'Why, she can hardly remember what he looks like.'

'All the same, I think we ought to make an effort. A change will be good for us all, especially for Giles, he's been here miles too long.'

Jack laughed.

'Be it as you please,' he said. 'But,' giving her his tawny glare, 'you may have to foot the bill.'

CHAPTER X

GILES and Charlotte had been communicating with each other for several years. This was a fact not unknown to either of their respective mothers, who scanned the handwriting on the outgoing and the incoming envelopes, and in both cases there was the post-mark for proof.

Both Judith and Hester had been brought up in the current tradition that in no case must a parent, especially a mother, interfere with her children's lives.

The way of parents was hard, harder perhaps, for fathers than for mothers. Fathers in family relationships were absolutely taboo: as far as their sons were concerned, they could not get it right, they could do no good, they could only do harm. If they tried to exercise discipline on the boy, they repressed him, disastrously curtailing his freedom of self-expression, from which arose many psychic traumas, ranging in their effect from mild naughtiness to murder; if they let him go his own way they were 'accused' (a fashionable word) of neglecting him, and of letting him become a hippy, a thug, a skinhead, a hooligan or something worse. Mothers were 'accused' of neglecting their children by selfishly going out to work; whereas fathers, who also went out to work, were 'accused' of corrupting their progeny's (male and female) entire nature simply by repressing, or failing to repress, their natural instincts.

Love was another factor. Many writers about the relationship of parents and children emphasized the importance of love. Without love, children wouldn't get anywhere, anywhere desirable, that is; they would soon find themselves in Borstal, heading for a career of crime. But another school said that children did not want 'security' (another cant word of the time) and above all, they didn't want *love*. Love was abhorrent to them because, if over-emphasized, it checked, or might check, their natural and inevitable desire for freedom of self-expression. Love, love as a therapeutic for adolescent ills, was utterly archaic.

Naturally, both Judith and Hester had taken these matters into account when bringing up Charlotte and Giles. But there was a great difference between their attitudes, although psychiatrists might have thought it superficial: Judith had plenty of money, while Hester had very little. Yet through all the years since Grandad Handforth's death, Charlotte and Giles had maintained a desultory correspondence, and kept in touch with what was happening to each of them.

Giles received a letter with his invitation:

'Dearest Giles,

I wish I could have been with you for the sheep-shearing—I know I should have enjoyed it and it's such ages since I was at Helvellyn Farm. I wish Aunt Hester would have asked me. But even if she had I couldn't have come, for we were having a party here in our new house—the old one was much too small and Grandad's was old-fashioned and inconvenient, so we sold it, as you know. This new one is the tops! It's in a much nicer part of the town for one thing, and has quite a big garden, though not too big—and a wonderful drawing-room. We had a dance for twenty-five couples, would you believe it? and it didn't seem a bit crowded. And then we had supper in the dining-room—five round tables—that *was* a bit of a squash, but of course they didn't all come in at the same time.

We had the food brought in from outside, I have to confess, and a professional waiter to help Angiolina—he looked so smart that some people thought he was one of the guests! But it makes such a difference when there is someone to *wait*, don't you think? And he slid about between the tables like an eel.

The only sad thing was that you weren't there. Mummy didn't think you'd really enjoy it, as most of them would have been strangers to you, and it's such a long way for you to come—though we could have put you up for the night, and the house is peppered with loos and bathrooms. But I do hope you will be able to come for my birthday which is our *real* housewarming—it will be too sad if you can't.

Ever your loving,
Charlotte.'

Giles showed this letter to his mother, and she showed it to his father.

'I really think we must make the effort,' she said. 'We may be only their country cousins, but we don't want to lose touch with them, do we? Charlotte's letter is boastful, I know, but what can you expect of a girl of her age, whose parents have a lot of money to throw about? Seymour isn't my favourite man, any more than he's yours—he's so sleek and dapper and self-contained—but Judith is my sister, whatever we think about her influence on Daddy.'

'Does Giles know about that?' Jack asked.

'No, and I think it's better that he shouldn't. It might put him off Charlotte who, however worldly she may have become, is clearly still fond of him, and I think it does her credit, when she has all these attractive young men milling around.'

'Does Giles know that she's still fond of him?' Jack asked. 'He doesn't seem very keen on girls.'

'Perhaps not, but they are always writing to each other, and may be he will one day.'

'Do you think marriage between cousins is a good idea?'

Hester knit her brows.

'It often works, doesn't it? And Giles is a boy who needs encouragement.'

'Do you think Judith and Seymour would fancy him as a son-in-law?'

'Perhaps not. He certainly hasn't got the makings of a money-spinner, but Charlotte will have plenty of the wherewithal, and considering the way young people go on nowadays, Judith and Seymour may think they may as well be hung for a lamb as a sheep.'

Jack laughed.

'Which do you think Giles is?'

'He hasn't had time to show. He may turn out to be a lion, like you are.'

Not ill-pleased with the compliment, Jack stretched out his paws, and said:

'Well, if you want to go, Hester, let's go.'

'I don't want to go, Heaven knows,' said Hester indignantly, 'but I think that for Giles's sake perhaps we should. You have your Sunday suit—'

'I don't wear it on Sundays,' interrupted Jack.

'No, because you don't go to Church—I only wish you would. I have, as you say, my black outfit, and there's a little woman in Carlisle who might make it presentable, and as for Giles, we'll have to see about him. Trousers can always be lengthened.'

'You don't want to make the poor boy look like a scarecrow, do you?' Jack asked. 'He's sensitive enough as it is, and he'll be worse if you make him look a figure of fun.'

'Well,' said Hester, 'I don't want them to think we are all rolling in money, do you? We might have been better off if Judith hadn't—well, I don't know! Giles is the problem—he'll have to have another suit for Speech Day, in any case, so he might as well get it now. He hates to have a suit tried on—I don't know why, but he wriggles and protests as if he was being put into a strait-jacket, and when the tailor has pins in his mouth it drives him frantic.'

'Most children are neurotic nowadays,' said Giles's father, tolerantly.

'Yes, but we want him to look his best, don't we? And make a good impression on Charlotte and the rest of them, however much they may have soared above our social station.'

'Well, have it your own way,' said Jack, 'but don't blame me if you feel like a fish out of water.'

'Believe me, I shan't,' said Hester.

CHAPTER XI

GILES didn't know he had been the subject of his parent's conversation, still less did he know that but for him the invitation to Charlotte's birthday party might not have been accepted. He wanted to see Charlotte, but the idea of parties frightened him—he was unused to them, they were so uncommon in that part of Cumberland.

But when his mother told him what he already knew, but which came with added force from her lips, that Charlotte wanted to see him and would be unhappy if he didn't go, he tried to overcome his fears, especially his fears of being inadequate to the social situation—a country boy, probably incorrectly dressed, with two or three dozen total strangers round him, all knowing each other but not knowing him. He saw himself among a crowd of alien faces, all intent on each other, all smiling at each other, but with no recognition of him.

But having been brought up on such sayings as 'Nothing turns out as bad as you think it will' and (perhaps more encouraging) 'You never died in winter yet,' he agreed to the visit, as indeed he would have had to, as his parents seemed to be set on it and he was by no means a rebellious boy.

But oh, the tightening in his chest, the flutterings in his stomach, and the liquefaction in his lower regions, as mile by mile and hour by hour they drew nearer to the torture-chamber! Sitting in front with his father (his mother, in the car at any rate, preferred the back seat), he marvelled how his father could remain so unconcerned—intent, it seemed, on the means of arriving, not on the ultimate destination of the journey. As with so many men, he became fiercer when driving; he frowned, he scowled, his profile stiffened. Every now and then he would mutter some smothered imprecation at a passing or overtaking driver who, as he thought, had transgressed some rule of the road.

And every now and then Giles would guiltily hope that they might meet with a *small* accident (not their fault, of course, but the fault of one of those reckless drivers) which would prevent them from proceeding further and turn them on their homeward track.

Nothing of this sort happened and towards the close of an autumn day they found themselves, after several inquiries as to the exact location of Havant, turning up the gravel sweep and alighting, stiff and weary, at the front door.

Even Giles's apprehensions were somewhat stilled by the relief of arrival.

And oh, what a welcome they received; Judith and Seymour and Charlotte were at the door, with the bright light of a converted carriage lamp overhead, and behind them a ruddy glow, in which a maid lurked. Kisses and embraces were exchanged; Charlotte, whom Giles hardly recognized after so many years, clung to him and showered him with endearments. Then all four advanced to take the visitor's luggage, but Jack insisted on carrying his and Hester's; 'Women always travel so *heavy*,' he complained and explained. Then they were escorted up to their rooms.

'You must be dreadfully tired,' said Judith.

'Oh, not at all,' said Jack. 'But there are always some fools on the road who make driving more difficult than it need be.'

*

'Do you and Jack like separate rooms, or separate beds, or do you prefer to "muck in together"?' asked Judith, putting the last question into the heaviest of inverted commas. 'Oh, we muck in together,' said her sister. 'We should feel lonely if we didn't.

The Will and the Way

'Well, then, here you are,' said Judith, ushering them into their bedroom, the top-light of which dazzled them after the faint, unwilling electric light of their own home.

'And here is the bathroom.' She indicated to the left. 'Not quite what we would have wished, but still! And there's an electric heater, if the central heating isn't up to its job.'

Voices were heard outside the door.

'That must be Charlotte and Giles,' said Judith, 'What a bad hostess I am, to leave him to the tender mercies of my daughter, fond as she is of him! I dare say she doesn't know where his room is, though young people,' she added reflectively, 'know so much nowadays.' She hurried out, and they heard her voice mingling with the lighter voices of the youngsters. There was silence; and then Judith, coming back, said, 'I've shown Giles his room. I'm afraid he hasn't a bathroom—we couldn't fit in another—but there is one almost opposite. I hope he won't mind.'

'I'm sure he won't,' his father said rather tersely. 'He has to fit into our bathroom whenever he gets the chance. It rains a lot in our district, but funnily enough, our tank doesn't always get filled up.'

'Would you like Charlotte to help him to unpack?' Judith asked. 'I'm sure she would like to.'

The cousins' voices could still be heard outside the door, rising and falling, chiming and counter-chiming, almost musically.

'I don't think he's got much to unpack,' said Jack, embarrassed. 'Just what he's standing up in, and he can't unpack *that*'—he smiled down at Judith with his self-excusatory look—'and the suit we got for him to wear for Charlotte's birthday party to-morrow. Hester chose it—I don't think he altogether liked it—boys don't always like their clothes being chosen for them—I didn't myself.'

Judith looked up at him and envied, not for the first time, his stature and his random good looks, of which he seemed so unselfconscious. 'I've brought my good suit—it's the only decent suit I have, and I hope it won't disgrace you.'

'My dear boy,' she began, and stopped. 'Where are we? Where is everybody?'

She bustled out of the room, and her voice was heard in accents cooing, commanding, entreating, adapting itself to the various requirements of the new house, and the over-bright lights, which shone in all the rooms.

'And where is Seymour?' her voice was suddenly heard, calling from an adjacent passage. 'Seymour, where are you?'

A faint voice, like the echo of a voice, answered from the interior.

'Seymour, come here!'

Judith was standing on the landing, the main landing, at the top of the staircase ornamented with prints of battles—The Nile, Copenhagen, the glorious First of June, and the last but greatest, the cockpit of the *Victory* at Trafalgar—when Seymour, slight, suave, dark-haired and looking younger than his forty-five years, appeared between the two terrestrial, and celestial, globes which he and Judith had kept when they sold the contents of her father's house.

'Yes, darling?'

'Nothing, nothing—Hester and Jack and Giles are here, as you know, and we're just going to have supper. But I thought you would like to give them a drink beforehand. They've come a very long way to be at Charlotte's birthday party.'

'Of course, of course,' he said, casting his dark glance up at her, 'The drinks are all ready in the ante-room.'

'Then shall we ring the gong?' said his wife. 'They may not be used to it, but at any rate it won't frighten them. I expect they have changed, as much as they mean to change. You and I can stay as we are.' They surveyed each other. 'It's a bore, isn't it? But then relations are a bore.'

*

Jack and Hester had cudgelled their brains for something that Charlotte might be without, and that (more difficult still) she might *want*. Jack's suggestions, starting with a lambswool coat, gave out very quickly. Hester knit her brows. 'I'm not sure if they wear them now—fashions change so quickly.' At last she had written to her sister, asking if she could think of something Charlotte may like. Judith replied at once that Charlotte hoped to go ski-ing in the Christmas holidays; and that any contribution to that would be more than welcome. Hester made inquiries; and it appeared that only a complete ski-ing outfit would do as a present. Any particular details might not agree with others. Having committed herself, Hester did not feel she could draw back; a complete ski-ing outfit it must be.

When he heard what it would cost, Jack groaned.

'But they never give Giles anything—I don't believe they remember when his birthday is, or if he has one. They gave him a safety-razor when he was twelve, as if he needed to shave at that age!'

'I have an idea it will come in useful,' said his mother darkly. 'Boys are so secretive—I have an idea he has brought it with him—in fact I know he has, because I saw it on his dressing-table. Quite a nice case, you know—I shouldn't know what the razor itself was like, or how much it cost.'

'I don't believe he shaves,' his father said, stroking his chin.

'No, because he's very fair, just as you are, Jack, and it wouldn't show.'

'It's quite possible he wanted to make an impression on Charlotte, who is younger than he is but maturer than he is. And he may have thought that she would come into his bedroom and think, "There's a man!"'

'Heaven forbid!' said Jack, twitching his broad shoulders.

'Well, these things have to happen, don't they? In my opinion Giles is as innocent as the babe unborn—but I'm not sure Charlotte is.'

'Do you think she fancies him?'

'I'm quite sure she does.'

'Well, he'll soon be old enough to marry, but whether he'll have enough to marry on is another matter, unless you and I retire into the poorhouse. Or cancel Charlotte's ski-ing outfit.'

'We can't, it's here already.'

'Don't you think,' said Jack, raising his tawny brows, 'that we pay more attention than we need to your in-laws? After all, what have they done for us?'

Hester said nothing.

'But they haven't done much for us, have they? I know that Judith did a great deal for your Dad that we couldn't do, and she knows, and always has known, on which side her bread was buttered—'

'Judith was very fond of my father,' Hester said.

'No doubt. But was that a good reason for leaving her four-fifths of his money when she was already married to a well-to-do man—? And yet we come down here to kow-tow to them, and give them presents we can't afford—'

'I think families should always stick together,' said Hester firmly. 'You never know when you may need them.'

'Well, I was an orphan,' Jack said, 'I had to make my own way in the world.' His voice apologized for this vainglorious assertion, and he added hastily, 'You know what I mean, Hester. After my parents died, my relations felt they had to look after me, blood is thicker than water, but they weren't very keen on it, and got rid of me as soon as they could, to be a shepherd-boy in Cumberland. That was how I met you, do you remember? I earned a few extra shillings a week as a paper-boy at a rather posh hotel where you and your Mum and Dad and your sister were staying, and we met and, well, you know what happened afterwards.'

'You needn't remind me,' Hester said. 'I remember it as well as you do.'

'And you remember how you asked me to write to you and I did—funny letters they must have been, for I was only a nipper, and got my education, such as it was, between sheep and school and newspapers—and then I met those chaps who were better off than me, but didn't work so hard, and we made a sort of

The Will and the Way

partnership. And then we went on writing to each other, and I met your Dad, and he seemed to take to me—'

'I know he did,' said Hester, 'but why are you telling me all this now?'

Jack blushed. It was a habit he couldn't overcome; the faint flush, hardly deepening his fair complexion, went to the roots of his blond hair.

'I dunno,' he said, with a colloquialism that Hester liked while she deplored it, 'except that we have come here for Charlotte's posh party, not because they wanted us, but because they felt they had to, and with the new house and everything—they sold your Dad's house for a packet—we shall be like fish out of water.'

Jack's face had a remarkable range of expressions; he could look sad and happy at the same time: the shepherd-boy and the newspaper boy, with their few praisings and their many scoldings and resentments, lingered in the man he was.

'I know what you mean,' Hester said, 'you mean we're not up to their standard. We can't give a dance for thirty people, or however many there are coming in after dinner. Judith has her faults —I know them well. She wants to make a splash in the social world of Middlehampstead with her money, and the money Seymour has made since. Oh yes, they are quite well off, thanks to Dad's Will, and we aren't.'

'For all that, Charlotte seems fond of Giles,' Jack said.

'Yes, but what do children know about money? As a woman, I know what Charlotte feels about Giles—she likes the promise of manliness' (she glanced at her husband) 'that he's had before his time. He isn't town-bred; he's beginning to have those large hands and swelling wrists that you have, and they appeal to a certain type of woman. Not that he's aware of it, I'm sure.'

'I should hope not,' said Jack, looking down with disfavour on his exaggerated extremities. 'You wouldn't want to dance with a gorilla.'

'Who can say?' said Hester, laughing. '*Chacun à son goût*. But I know that Charlotte has a *penchant* for Giles, poor as he is, and she always has had.'

A gong sounded through the house. 'That's to warn us to get ready for dinner,' said Hester hastily. 'Father always did it, and they've kept the practice up. Now where is Giles?'

'You'd better go and find out,' said her husband. 'I'm going to have a bath,' he added, looking eagerly at their bathroom door. 'We don't have this luxury in Cumberland, do we, Hester?'

•

The dinner when it came, so different to the heaped-up platefuls on the kitchen-table which Giles was used to, appearing course after course, handed round by Angiolina with her impassive face, left them awe-struck. And the candles on the table, reflecting their light from the gleaming mahogany, the lighting subdued, in some strange manner, behind the cornices in the ceiling, the whole room aglow—it was too much for Giles, who was sensitive to his surroundings, and if he hadn't had Charlotte sitting next to him and could watch her dealing with the dishes at their menacing approach, he might not have been able to eat anything at all.

But even while she patronized him, indeed the more she patronized him, she was determined to be nice to him, her country cousin whom it was such fun to introduce into the ways of polite society—not condescending to him, but approaching him as a pet whom she wanted to house-train.

Giles flourished under her affectionate tutelage, for he was far from vain, indeed, too apprehensive in these grand surroundings to harbour a vain thought of vanity; moreover he knew, with the instinctive knowledge of his age, that she was not trying to take the mickey out of him, but (if there is such a phrase) to put the mickey in. Thus the party, the birthday party tomorrow, was to be as much for him as for her.

'The others won't count half as much as you do,' she said. 'You won't be nervous, will you, of so many strangers? They'll like you all the better because you come from so far away. I know several who are longing to meet you, besides several you already know.'

So she tried to wean him from his fears with all sorts of little gestures and exclamations that were new to her parents and new to her. Her mother began to give her sidelong looks; she was not anxious for this boy-and-girl friendship to ripen into a warmer feeling; there were so many other and larger pebbles on the beach than Giles. She was quite fond of Giles, but he was only a poor relation, country-bred, and in every way unsuitable for Charlotte, who had already taken on some of the airs and mannerisms of the town and was using them, consciously or unconsciously, to captivate her cousin. Was he responding? Her mother couldn't tell. He was obviously flattered by her attentions, her town-bred wiles, just as she was pleased by his appearance and the suggestion of his father's vigour which underlay his growing frame. Yes, the attraction might be mutual, and if so it should be stopped before it went too far.

'Are you fond of dancing, Giles?' she asked him when dinner was over and he had helped, with vigorous puffs, to blow the candles out.

'Well, I'm afraid I don't know much about it,' he said, reddening. 'We don't have many dances in our part of the world.'

'Oh dear, what a pity,' Judith said. 'Charlotte is so fond of dancing. But you can sit with me, Giles, and keep me company while we watch the others.'

A sense of inadequacy, of defeat almost, overcame Giles at that moment. It was almost purely personal and unrelated to Charlotte; but what is the use of living, he asked himself, if one couldn't dance? To be a wall-flower—and the picture of a wall-flower sitting, or worse still, growing next to his Aunt Judith, whom he had never much liked, for hours and hours and hours sickened him. The whole prospect of the visit, which he had secretly dreaded for many weeks, sickened him. The rich dinner which he had forced down into his stomach, against his stomach's inclination, sickened him. Dreadful physical symptoms, remembered from long ago, began to arise; was he *going* to be sick?

Just as that moment he heard Charlotte's voice, coming from afar, borne on the wings of health.

'Of course, Mummy, it doesn't matter whether Giles can dance or not. I shall have all this evening to teach him, and all tomorrow morning, and all tomorrow afternoon, between tea and dinner, and then he'll know *everything*, at least everything *I* know.'

Her mother didn't look too well pleased.

'Of course, if you think dancing can be learnt as soon as that—'

'Oh, but it depends on who's learning it,' said Charlotte, giving Giles a loving look. 'Now Daddy could never learn to dance'—she glanced across at him from her chair to his—'because you never *loved* it, did you, Daddy? You've often said so.'

There was an uncomfortable pause.

'Your father,' said Judith, looking at the room with its rich furnishings and addressing the company as if they were all his children, 'has had other things to think of.'

Seymour Snape closed his eyes, an evasive habit he had when Judith asked him too direct a question.

'I don't think so, my dear,' he answered mildly. 'I like to see young people dance, but my dancing days are over.'

CHAPTER XII

THE next day went much as Charlotte meant it should—that is to say, in intensive dancing instructions for Giles. Needless to say, he resented them; and needless to say he was flattered by them. One or two of the dances involved bodily contact; one or two kept each partner at a distance, foot-active and gesturing towards each other. Charlotte, the expert, was wise enough to realize that Giles, even if he had been Nureyev himself, couldn't take in, and construe with appropriate action, more than a few movements. She also realized what instructors and instructresses in many of the arts do not, that he would be bored by having to repeat them. So she contented herself with saying, after this or that movement in which Giles was either facing or embracing her or even turning his back on her, that he had done it very well.

And this was not altogether untrue; for Giles had a natural agility, derived from his father and his own activities on the lakeland fells. He could make the wrong movement, but like a boy on a Greek vase, he could not make an awkward one. Charlotte was just as pleased herself with his performance as she allowed herself to appear; she stimulated in him many capacities that he did not know he possessed; and he sat down to dinner feeling almost as confident as she wanted him to be.

Four favoured guests had been asked to dinner and while they assembled for drinks, ten of them all told, in Mr. Snape's study (standing room only), birthday presents were offered and received by Charlotte with screams of delight. It is always an anxious moment when one submits a present, especially a present to a girl or woman who probably has all she wants already.

Alas, alas. The male guests all wore dinner-jackets; even Mr. Holroyd had one, bought long ago for some forgotten occasion, but still fitting him as everything he wore fitted him; only Giles was singular in his dark suit; his parents, on economy bent, had thought he wasn't old enough to need a dinner-jacket. Giles was acutely conscious of his sartorial insufficiency, especially in regard to the length of his sleeves. His suit had been bought off the peg, and had seemed to fit him; it was only when he stretched his arms out for the salt or the pepper that he was aware how much his red wrists showed. In vain he pulled his sleeves down; with each surreptitious tug they seemed, with the well-known malice of inanimate objects, to reveal more of him than ever.

His companions on the right and left, neither of whom he knew, did not seem to notice his distress, but no doubt they were too well brought up to do so. Opposite him was Charlotte, with on each side of her a dashing young man, rather older than himself in age and much older in experience. She was talking to one of them; the other was talking to his mother; the family and the visitors made up ten. But what struck Giles most, and what hurt him most, was the perfect sleeve-lengths of the young men opposite him; never, whatever gesture they made, did they reveal more than an inch of wrist and half-an-inch of a jewelled cuff-link.

*

Later in the evening, the after-dinner guests began to arrive, to the number of twenty at least, each bringing with him or her a birthday gift for Charlotte. Sometimes it was, most inconveniently, a bunch of flowers which had hastily to be thrust into whatever vase was left over to contain them; sometimes it was a box of chocolates; sometimes it was blessedly small, a bottle of scent or bath essence which Charlotte and her parents, who were receiving the guests, could place decoratively on the hall table. A few of the guests brought no presents at all, but scurried past, looking small, into the big white music-room, round which and for which the house had been built. Already the strains of music could be heard tuning up from the far end when a late, indeed the latest, guest arrived, bringing a present in an exquisite little box. He didn't look round him when the hired man took his elegant cloak from off his shoulders; he didn't ask for or receive a ticket; he bowed slightly to Charlotte, with an air of someone too well known to need a more formal introduction.

'Take Marcus in to join the others, will you?' her mother said. 'I don't think anyone else will be coming now.'

The dancing had indeed already begun and he, as though by right, had the first dance with her.

Meanwhile Giles, bewildered by the bright lights and wondering how to dispose of himself, spied his mother sitting on a gilt chair by the wall and made for her.

'Do you think I need dance?' he asked. 'I would much rather not. Do you think I could slip away?'

His mother glanced at her plain gold wrist-watch, which showed a few minutes after ten.

'I should stay a little longer, dearest, if you can bear it,' she said. 'I think Aunt Judith would be disappointed if you didn't, and Charlotte would be disappointed too.'

Giles glanced at Charlotte, who was posturing, expertly and provocatively, in front of the late-comer Marcus, whose name Giles did not know, but whose gestures of head, shoulders, arms, body and legs were keeping a sort of rhythm with hers, although they weren't looking at each other.

'Charlotte's the belle of the ball,' he said, essaying this daring expression, 'and I do feel she would be happier if I was out of the way—that is, if she notices I'm in it.' He smiled.

'You mustn't judge things too much at first sight,' his mother said, 'I used to go to dances as a girl, and I remember that they didn't always begin as they ended.' She stole a glance at Jack who, gilt-chair-seated, was trying to make conversational headway with a woman whom he evidently didn't know. 'At dances things don't always end as you expect,' she went on vaguely, 'and I think Charlotte would be disappointed, after all the trouble she has taken, if she doesn't have a dance or two with you.'

'But I've already forgotten the steps she taught me,' Giles protested. 'And if she wanted to dance with me, why is she dancing with that chap over there, who dances better than I ever could in a month of Sundays and looks so smart? I should only make us both look fools.'

'Then why did Charlotte take so much time and trouble to give you dancing-lessons?' his mother asked, 'if she didn't want to dance with you?'

Giles saw the logic in this, but the evening party had put him so much out of love with himself and with his surroundings—if only these smart young people had been sheep waiting to be sheared!

'Oh, I don't know, Mother. I suppose she has to fill in her time like anyone else—and take up mine,' he added, with a bitterness that was quite foreign to him.

'Be patient, be patient,' his mother said, half imploring, half commanding. 'You'll have much worse things to go through than this.' She smiled, and he tried to smile back. 'There'll be a change in a minute or two, nothing ever stays the same for long,' she added, with a sadness in her voice that her son recognized but did not understand.

'Now be a good boy and wait for a minute or two.'

Giles waited, and when the music stopped the couples, in so far as they were engaged, disengaged themselves and made for the chairs by the walls; but hardly had the three-piece band struck up again when he saw, to his amazement and dismay, his mother and father taking the floor, clinging together in an old-fashioned style, to the strains of the Blue Danube.

Soon other couples joined them; and the floor was alive again with dancing feet.

It hadn't occurred to Giles, sitting alone between three or four empty chairs, that his parents were young enough to dance.

More than once they passed by him in his isolation and smiled down at him, intent on their own happiness, though not forgetful of him; but just as the room had become for him a desert of well-dressed demons he felt rather than saw somebody sitting down beside him, and Charlotte said, 'I know it isn't for me to say it, but may I have the pleasure?'

Giles jumped to his feet, hardly aware that it was she, so enclosed had he been in his isolation.

'Of course,' he said, feeling the dark mantle of solitude, like an invisible cloak, roll off him. 'But *can* I?'

'Yes, you can,' she replied, and the affirmation rang in his ears, louder and more potent than any he could have given himself. 'Yes, you can,' she repeated. 'Don't you remember how we practised it together, and how good you were at it?' And before he was aware of it, they were with each other and the other dancers, he not finding it difficult to follow the steps and rhythms of the waltz, so impulsive was their effect on his ear and so hypnotic the effect of Charlotte moving beside him.

'Shall we sit on the stairs?' she asked, when the dance was over. 'The stairs is the classic place to retire to at a dance, and only half-lit, while that music-room is a glare of light where you can't hear yourself speak or think. Does that sound nonsense?' she asked, drawing him close to her. 'And another thing is, Giles, that most of the guests don't really know where the staircase *is*, because this is the house's birthday as well as mine, and if they did know, they might think twice before they took root here. I see some of them *have*,' glancing with proprietorial disapproval of heads bent together and arms intertwined. She took Giles' hand and climbed a few steps higher. 'Now they can't see us, because they only want to look at each other, as we do, don't we, Giles?' and she turned on him a melting look which warmed, and lit up to the interior eye, the twilight between them.

He held her tight.

'I thought—' he began.

'What did you think?'

'Never mind what I thought,' he said, with a sudden access of masculine pride which thrilled through his arm round her waist. 'I thought,' he began again, and stopped. 'Isn't that the music for a new dance?'

'I suppose it is,' she said, not interested. 'I'm not sure if it's one you know. Shall we dance it together, or shall we just sit here?'

'Oh, let's sit here,' said Giles, whose fear of dancing, though on the one brief occasion he had enjoyed it, still haunted his mind. 'Let's stay here.'

Charlotte knit her brows and suddenly looked rather like her mother.

'It's the last dance,' she said. 'I think we ought to put in an appearance, being members of the family, and then there's supper, which we can have together if you like, Giles—and that's the end. Our parents will be disappointed if we don't. It's a *bal blanc* and stops at midnight, like Cinderella's.'

Reluctantly Giles followed her down the dimly-lit staircase and plunged, blinking, into the brilliant chandeliers and glowing wall-lights of the music room.

They might have been away for hours, Giles thought. He did his utmost to acquit himself well in this last dance, which demanded a degree of personal physical initiative that he was quite incapable of; and he had seldom felt happier than when the sweat-soaked musicians, working up to their final crescendo and accelerando, stopped.

Hardly recognizing each other, he and Charlotte made each other a bow. 'I think I see a table over there,' said Charlotte who, in common with other girls, and unlike men, did not sweat from prolonged physical exertion and kept their heads better than men, perhaps from less indulgence in alcohol.

'Over there, in that corner,' she said, indicating it.

On their way they brushed against Marcus, with a most lustrous girl on his arm. Passing Charlotte he raised his eyebrows, with a faint hint of complicity and reproach. She lowered hers and raised her shoulders.

Champagne, *foie gras*, chicken and the mousse to follow.

Giles could hardly keep his eyes open, but a new warmth of feeling for Charlotte stole across him, quite independent of his digestive processes.

He didn't remember what he said; he didn't remember what she said; but when there was a general movement in the room to signify that the company was departing, she whispered in his ear:

'You will marry me one day, won't you?'

'Of course I will,' he said, not for the first time.

CHAPTER XIII

TIME passed and one morning a letter came, a formal card, saying:

Mr. & Mrs. Seymour Snape
have much pleasure in inviting
Mr. & Mrs. John Holroyd
to the marriage of their daughter Charlotte Patricia
to Marcus Neville
at St. Peter's, Eaton Square, London S.W.1
on Saturday, July 24th and afterwards at
Claridge's Hotel, London W.1.

Jack and Hester exchanged looks. 'And that will be an invitation for Giles,' said Hester, glancing at the letter at his place at the breakfast-table. This was one of the few days he was late.

Jack was the first to speak.

'It'll be a blow for the boy,' he said. 'He'd set his mind on Charlotte.'

'Not so much as she'd set her mind on him,' said Hester tartly. 'It dated from that birthday dance of Judith's, and before perhaps. Cousins—' She didn't finish what she meant to say.

'Cousins or no cousins,' said Jack, to whose looks the north country climate and his way of life had been kind, 'I think she's done him a dirty trick.'

'Who has?' asked Hester.

'Charlotte, of course.'

'Why do you think Charlotte? Much more likely Judith.'

Jack sat back in his chair. He didn't understand these female wiles.

'Well, it's Charlotte's affair.'

'Not so much as it's Judith's.'

'Why is it Judith's?'

'How *can* you ask, Jack? This man Marcus is very well off; his family is very well off; he's what you might call a catch.'

Jack thought for a while.

'And has Charlotte no say in it? I thought she was really fond of our boy. I know he was fond of her; he's twenty-two now, and he would have found another girl if he hadn't been. Why, I wasn't twenty when you and I were married.'

'Yes, but we married for love,' said Hester, getting up to remove their breakfast plates. 'Judith wants Charlotte to marry for money, that's the difference.'

'I should have thought that Judith and Seymour had plenty,' said Jack.

'Yes, but the more you have, the more you want.'

Jack heaved a sigh and spread out his broad shoulders. Was love sufficient recompense to a woman, he asked himself in a sudden moment of introspection, for a remote, isolated life, with very little money and no social life to spend that little on? The look he gave Hester expressed this feeling; and she did not misunderstand.

'Ah, but we were precocious,' said Jack, jocular.

'So we might have been,' said Hester, facing him across their empty places on the table-cloth, 'but we had no one to come between us—at least I hadn't, but I can't answer for you.'

'Well, it's different for a man,' said Jack with a somewhat complacent smirk.

'Oh yes, you all say that. But at any rate—' She stopped.

'You mean that Giles has had no feminine interest other than Charlotte?'

'Only when he's been looking after the ewes.'

Jack laughed.

'In my experience, ewes don't keep a man from looking outside the sheepfold. They didn't keep me. So why Giles? Or do you keep tabs on him?'

'Of course not,' answered Hester indignantly. 'But a mother knows, and I know that Giles and Charlotte have been close to each other since they were children—perhaps more on her side than his—and it's only because—'

'Because what?'

Hester drew a long breath.

'Sometimes, Jack, I think you're very dense. It's because Judith wants Charlotte to marry for money and we're too poor and have to keep a pupil, a lodger, to make both ends meet—'

'Philip is a nice boy and gets on well with Giles.'

'That has nothing to do with it,' said Hester, looking resentfully at Giles's and Philip's empty places. 'They really ought to get up earlier. It's eight o'clock—'

'Boys are always like that,' said Jack, tolerantly. 'Early to bed, late to rise—'

'I don't know about early to bed. But they might be more considerate. Phil reads a lot, he burns the midnight oil.'

'Yes, I know, and I like him and we couldn't get on without him, but perhaps he's mistaken his vocation. What I meant to say was—'

'Well?'

'Shall we accept this invitation to Charlotte's wedding? It will mean a wedding present. Well, we needn't spend much on that—they will have everything they want. But it's the journey, and the tiredness, and I don't really feel up to it. Do you?'

'I don't mind,' Jack said.

'Perhaps not—you're just a package, and all the organization will fall on me—you haven't even got a wedding-present, or one of those hats.'

'I should wear my dark suit.'

'But what about me? I should have to buy a new outfit, and so would you. No, we won't go.'

'I suppose they'll be offended,' Jack said.

'Well, let them be. What have they done for us? Nothing, and less than nothing.'

She heard a noise and hesitated. 'Was that them coming downstairs?'

The sound ceased.

Hester's anger increased and her colour rose.

'You know how Judith got hold of Daddy's money? More than four-fifths of what he left us?'

'I heard something,' Jack said.

'And do you know why he left it to her?'

'We can't do anything about that now,' said Jack. 'The Will has been proved, the money has been distributed, and it's just too bad. Forget it!'

'I would have forgotten it if it hadn't been for this last thing. Giles was in love with Charlotte, I know he was, and she was in love with him. They would have been ideally happy—ideally happy. She would have had enough money for them both—I don't care about that. But Judith was so socially and so money-wise ambitious that she persuaded Charlotte to marry this rich Marcus—there's nothing a mother can't do if she sets her mind on it.'

'Giles will find someone else,' said Jack.

'But will he? But will he? All his thoughts, his loving thoughts, were centred on Charlotte, and hers on him. It's a tragedy, Jack, it's a tragedy. And I've a good mind to tell him the story—of how his aunt, from sheer snobbery and greed of money, has deprived him of the happiness he would have had with Charlotte.'

'And what about Charlotte?'

'Well, we know, don't we? Charlotte is going to marry her rich *parti* Marcus. Good luck to them both. But I'm not going to the wedding, and I don't think you will want to. And what's more—'

'Is there anything more?' asked Jack.

'Yes, there is. I mean to tell Giles how all this came about.'

'No, don't do that.'

'I shall, not only because I don't ever want to speak to Judith again, but because I want him to forget Charlotte *altogether*. Oh, I hear the boys now, they're coming down to breakfast at last.'

CHAPTER XIV

'AND you don't want me to send her a wedding-present?' Giles asked.

'It's not what I want, it's what you want,' his mother said. 'I shouldn't want to, if I was in your place.'

'Are you and Daddy going to send her a present?'

'We might send her an ice-container—it depends how much they cost.'

Giles cast about in his mind. 'What could *I* give her?'

'Well,' said his mother tartly, 'You know her better than I do. What about a paperweight? They are very useful and can be quite expensive, if you want to give her something expensive.'

'I can't afford anything expensive—just something she might like.'

'Well, why not an address-book? They can be very decorative and pretty, and if she doesn't use them to write letters to you, she can use them for someone else. I know a place where you can get them.'

Giles pondered over this.

'I'm not really angry with her,' he said.

'But I don't suppose you're pleased with her,' said Hester, her long-controlled indignation mounting in the defence of her son. 'At any rate, I'm not. How long have you been friends with Charlotte? How long has she been having you on? Twelve years?'

'Oh, I don't know,' said Giles, whose mutual affection with Charlotte couldn't be counted in terms of years.

'I think it's longer than that,' said his mother. 'You are twenty-two—six months older than Charlotte. Put her out of your mind,

Giles, for God's sake, do. She isn't worth it. She's under her mother's thumb. If she could find a man better off than Marcus, Judith would make her marry him tomorrow.'

'Then you won't be going to the wedding?'

'Certainly not!'

'And you'd rather I didn't?'

'Oh, Giles, that's for you to decide—you are of age, as they say. If you want to go to the wedding of a girl—a woman, I suppose I should say—who has kept you on tenterhooks for I don't know how many years and then chucked you for a man who is better off—well, go by all means.'

'I think she is really fond of me, or she was. We've written to each other every week since—' he stopped.

'All the more reason to say goodbye to her now,' said his mother, who felt more deeply about this than Giles had any idea of. 'She was always a spoilt child and her mother Judith—my sister—did her best to spoil her.'

'You don't think Charlotte was really fond of me?' Giles asked, with a catch in his voice.

'I think she was quite fond of you,' said his mother, 'so long as no one better than you presented himself. Let us be frank, Giles. I never liked the idea of cousins marrying but while Daddy and I were fairly well off (or so Judith thought) she was quite keen on your marrying Charlotte. Then she and Seymour went up in the world, they met all sorts of well-to-do people, including this Marcus, and well, you know what's happened.'

'I still think she was fond of me,' said Giles.

'Yes, I'm sure she was, and she probably still is, in spite of her marriage to Marcus. But Judith has a will of iron—she wouldn't let Charlotte marry the son of a sheep-farmer in Cumberland.'

Giles wished he could get out of the room; the thought of those weekly letters, over months and years, with their love and kisses and child-like endearments, was almost more than he could bear.

'They've asked me to the wedding,' he said, looking at the engraved card in front of him. 'Shall I say no?'

The Will and the Way

'I would, if I were you.'

'But I must send her a present.'

'Well, join in with us, Giles. A nice ice-box—Daddy won't grudge it you—and I'm sure it will come in useful; they will give heaps of cocktail parties.'

Giles, who had not been to a public-school or learned how to keep a straight face, began to cry.

'Don't worry, my darling,' she soothed him, 'there are better fish in the sea than ever came out of it.'

She stroked the back of his neck, an action which, as a little boy, he had always found comforting, but still, although now a grown man, with a figure and features like his father's, he could not restrain his tears.

His mother, too, wept for him, but inwardly; her tears were invisible. But, she thought, he needs taking out of himself, and out of Charlotte, that hussy, who has led him on, and then let him down, whereas—she tried to think, without success, of girls in the district who might have taken, or might take, Charlotte's place.

His tears, which he did his best to stifle with fingers in his eyes, and when they were irrepressible, with a handkerchief, moved her so much that she said:

'Now listen, Giles. I can't feel for you more than I do, but let me tell you you are wasting your feelings on people who are not worthwhile. My father was a good man, but for one reason and another he was under the influence of my sister Judith. She persuaded him that she was a pauper, and she persuaded him to leave most of the money that he should have divided between us to *her*, although she knew perfectly well, she knew perfectly well, that she and Seymour had a fortune coming to them. And it has come. And that is why Charlotte is going to marry Marcus.'

Hester took a long breath and watched the effect this revelation would have on Giles. She was not altogether disappointed; he changed colour, he suddenly looked much older; he was obviously trying to adapt his family feelings of the years before to his present feelings—the feelings his mother had engendered in him.

'And did Charlotte know about this?' he asked.

'Of course she knew. She knew the terms of her grandfather's Will just as well as we know it.'

'You didn't tell me this before?'

'No, because—because—'

'And that is why Charlotte wanted to marry him—because they are well off and we aren't?'

'Yes, Giles,' his mother said. 'That is the main reason. I don't say that Charlotte isn't still fond of you—I dare say she is—but Marcus is a better catch.'

Hester has succeeded. Giles's tears had dried up—thought overcoming emotion. 'Hullo, Phil,' he said to his companion, 'it's time we started off.'

'I've been waiting for you,' Phil said, 'I thought you were never coming out of the kitchen.'

CHAPTER XV

WEEKS passed, then an unexpected letter came from Charlotte:

'Dearest Giles,
What must you think of me? But if you knew what I have been through in these last weeks you would feel sorry for me, even if you could not excuse me or love me. We were meant for each other, I knew that before you did, and still know it.

Mummy has her virtues, but she also has her faults—which she shares with Daddy. They would not hear of my marrying you, although they well knew how much I wanted to—perhaps more than you wanted to marry me—but don't let's go into that. But living as you do, far away in an isolated place with only sheep round you (no offence meant), you can have no idea what it's like in a provincial town like ours, where everyone knows everyone else's business and what their prospects are in the marriage market. And Mummy and Daddy are foremost in all this. In one way and another they have accumulated a lot of money, and I can't tell you the pressure they have put on me to marry Marcus—even to the point of saying that if I don't they will cut me off—not with the proverbial shilling, but with just a pittance, which you and I could live on, I suppose, but whether I should make a good wife to a sheep-farmer I rather doubt, having been brought up so differently—I mean in such different surroundings.

You see I am being as objective as I can, for both our sakes. I'm not being cruel, am I? And you don't feel that I love you less than I did?

My Aunt Hester married your father for love, for love of him and for love of his looks—she didn't care that he had no money to speak of and lived in an outlandish place—nor would I, dear Giles—at least I don't think so. But if you realized how they have put pressure on me every day to do what they want me to do, you would know how tired I am, so tired that I have given way to them.

I'm not in love with Marcus, though I have always liked him; but he's not a man after my own heart, and what's more he never will be. We can keep up appearances, but is there any reason we should do more than that? Wives and husbands are not chained together by iron bonds; we can get loose, legally or illegally.

If this shocks you, dearest Giles, say so, otherwise I shall hope that our friendship and our love for each other will continue—for there are always ways and means.

> Your ever devoted,
> Charlotte.'

Every day Giles felt he ought to answer this letter, and every day he put off doing so. There was more than one reason for his hesitation. He did not know what his own feelings were. One day he would be furious with her for her cruelty and never want to see her again; the next day he would remember their childhood friendship which ripened insensibly into love, seldom as the sun came from behind the distant clouds to shine on it. At such times he would long to see her, just as much as at other times he hated the idea.

Sometimes he thought it was inexcusably forward of her to have made the proposal she had made; sometimes he thought it was admirable and touching that she pocketed her pride when she was obviously in a position to keep it and forget all about him.

Had he ever offered her marriage? No, because he hadn't enough money and no likelihood of having it. Somehow he had hoped that they would some time come together, for his thoughts of her were almost as potent as her presence; but he had to admit

The Will and the Way

that she, who was getting on for twenty-two, could not feed her desires on the mere thought of his presence.

Since the present of the ice-container, a gift from all three, had been acknowledged, there had been no further communication, other than Charlotte's unanswered letter, between the two families; it was assumed that all relations between them were broken off.

Wrath is an exciting stimulant, but not a good companion, and though he didn't know why, Giles suffered from the poverty of his emotional life.

CHAPTER XVI

'You're not looking quite yourself today,' said Phil, when they were together on the fells.

'No, I'm not,' said Giles.

'What is it?' asked Phil, as they surmounted the rise and observed the tails of the sheep greedily looking forward to their next, indeed their continuing meal.

'It's Charlotte. Married to a town-bred chap. I don't think she's mad on him—but there it is. He has the wherewithal.'

Together they watched the agile black-tailed mountain-sheep, so familiar with their surroundings, scuttling over the next rise. They hastened their footsteps and called the shepherd-dog, awaiting their instructions.

'Rover, Rover!'

At once he came to heel with wagging tail, anxious to do their bidding. This they indicated to him, and after much barking and scurrying to and fro, with pretence bites at the ankles of the errant sheep, he had got them in, or nearly in, their pen.

'What are you going to do?' asked Phil when his arduous but necessary Georgic was almost over.

'Only this,' said Giles, panting up the slope of which the fleet-footed mountain sheep made nothing. 'Charlotte has gone back on me after all these years.' He started to explain. 'But you know it all, Phil.'

'Is there anything I can do?' Phil asked, with an eye to the last of the stragglers reluctantly returning to the flock.

'What can you do?'

The Will and the Way

'Do you want to break up their marriage?'

'I don't know what I want,' said Giles violently. 'I know I don't want them to be happy together—how can I?'

Philip considered this.

'Would you like me to put a spoke in their wheel?'

'I might.'

'Would you mind that?'

'No, certainly not,' said Giles, whose feelings during the last hour had completely got the better of him.

'And you wouldn't mind if I acted as a sort of go-between?'

'Do what you like,' said Giles, as they turned down the hill on to the ragged, unkempt ground that divided his house from the still more ragged, unkempt hills that frowned round and down on it.

CHAPTER XVII

THE friendship between the two young men prospered, although they were, or perhaps because they were, so very different both in appearance and in mental outlook. Since his disappointment over Charlotte, which still haunted him with a sense of emptiness and loneliness and frustration, Giles more and more found a substitute for love in sheep-farming; if someone had called him the bell-wether of the flock, he would not have been offended. Philip liked Giles for his pallid Norse looks, his placid temperament and his readiness to give way if any occasion for disagreement arose between them—as it rarely did. Giles, under his father, was really the boss of the farm; but he never gave orders, he only made suggestions, with which Philip was quite ready to fall in. And if Giles was, technically, his superior and instructor, Giles knew quite well, and Philip knew quite well, that without Philip's financial aid the Holroyd household would be much handicapped —perhaps unable to carry on.

So they were each dependent on the other. But perhaps the advantage lay with Philip, who was financially independent. But he wanted a profession, or at any rate an occupation, and Jack and Hester and Giles hoped he would eventually decide to throw in his lot with them, although naturally they did not want to make this too obvious to him.

Giles liked his darksome colleague and also envied him his ability to be free, or more or less free, to do in life what he wanted. For instance he could (so Giles thought) marry his girl-friend Rosamond any day he chose; whereas he, Giles, had signally failed to marry Charlotte. But Giles did not realize that Philip's independence was a form of servitude; he, Giles, had no power of choice—circumstances had made him a sheep-farmer, and a sheep-farmer he would always be, with or without a wife; whereas Philip had so many ways open to him, wife-wise and career-wise. At the moment, farming was his occupation; his doctor had advised for him an open-air life; but it was not what he wanted, and he probably would not have stuck to it but for his friendship with Giles. His parents (he was their only child) lived in a cloudy world of their own, and though they were far from being neglectful of Philip's welfare, it was not very real to them in their private conversations, and they felt that almost anyone would be a better judge of what was good for him than they were—above all, a doctor. Health was the most important thing. From good health (they enjoyed it themselves, they took good care of it and it was really what they lived for) radiated everything one could possibly want, just as ill-health stultified and inhibited everything. They did not realize that their valetudinarianism was a straitjacket in which they were enclosed more closely and inextricably than they would have been in the arms of an illness, which so often releases, from very boredom, interests and undertakings which could not have been imagined without it. Illness was a stimulus that Philip's parents (protected by their carapace of hypochondria) never enjoyed: but Philip was a kind of extension of their ruling phobia. They felt his liability to instant mortality as acutely as they felt their own.

Philip, however, took a more robust view of himself than they did. True, he had had bronchitis and pneumonia, but these unpleasant experiences had only increased his desire to get outside them, not his craving to live within them.

His friendship with Giles was more a matter of chemical than intellectual affinity. They liked each other and enjoyed each other's company, but they did not discuss with each other abstract matters outside the scope of liking. Perhaps they would have liked each other less if they had, for Giles's mind was fixed more on what lay ahead in the farming field and the sheep-grazing pastures than on what was current in the world of ideas and politics. They each had a personal secret, revolving round a certain person. But this secret, in spite of the intimacy of their friendship at a certain level, they did not feel disposed to confide to each other.

To say that Philip was starved of intellectual companionship at the Holroyd's farm would be an exaggeration, but he missed it and, being a voracious reader, soon got through the small stock of books on the Holroyd's book-shelves, which odldy enough included a translation of the *Georgics*, one volume of which he had had to copy out at school as a punishment for some offence—five hundred lines, but better than getting expelled, which is still regarded by some people as a serious handicap in later life. Besides having to perform this laborious exercise, Philip was quite a good Latin scholar and he still remembered, if rather bitterly, the moving line:

'O fortunatos nimium sua si bona norint,
Agricolas!'

And when he felt discontented with his life on the farm he invoked it: 'Remember,' he told himself, 'You are only too lucky—if you knew your luck—to be a farmer's boy!'

But like many men with a tendency to tuberculosis Philip was highly sexed, just as Giles, who had no such tendency, was undersexed. To look at them side by side, one would have thought the opposite, but one would have been wrong.

Philip had a girl friend with whom he sometimes consorted, and whose relationship with him was a little like Giles's had been with Charlotte, except it was definitely more physical. Philip could have married Rosamond any day of the week, so far as money went, but there was an unspoken agreement between his parents that it would be best to wait till his health was established. Rosamond preferred not to wait until his doctor had given him a clean bill of health. She wanted security, social and personal, now; and

The Will and the Way

she did not believe in or care much about his doctor's misgivings. To Hell with him, she thought; let's get on with it!

Philip, although professionally in sheep, and perhaps a better judge of them as mutton-to-be than Giles, was not interested in them for themselves, but he sometimes took Rosamond (for he had a car of his own) to look at them from a distance.

'Aren't they too pretty? Think what Samuel Palmer would have made of them.'

'I only hope they'll make a lot for you!' said Rosamond, who was nothing if not practical.

'They are the only way of making us a happy marriage,' Philip said.

'Are they enough to make a happy marriage for Giles?'

'I'm a little unhappy about that boy,' Philip said, 'because he is still a boy, and if he waits any longer for his vision of a Charlotte to become a reality he may wait to be a hundred.'

'And so may others,' said Rosamond rather tartly.

'Yes, but we know where we stand, don't we? If you saw a chap more attractive than me, you would—it wouldn't be difficult—what I mean to say, Rosamond, if you met someone else—well, we shouldn't feel the world had come to an end, would we?'

'I see your drift,' said Rosamond, 'but what has this to do with your friend Giles and his problem?'

'Well, he doesn't see things the way we see them.'

CHAPTER XVIII

ONE day, when Philip and Giles were exploring the premises, some of them outdated and disused, as many farm buildings are and always have been, they went up into the granary.

'Good heavens,' said Philip, looking round the walls lined with books, though with no shelves to support them, 'where did all these come from?'

'They belonged to my grandfather, as a matter of fact,' said Giles, regarding the library with some distaste, 'and when he died and left his house to my Aunt Judith, she bequeathed his books to us. I don't know if she had them valued; I expect she did, and they didn't turn out to be worth much. Anyhow, here they are, and they are quite dry, unless they have got dry-rot. No-one has touched them and I don't suppose anyone will. They were meant to be a kind of—compensation.'

'A solatium?' suggested Philip.

'What does that mean?'

'Well, what you said. A minor recompense for a major injury.'

'Well, you are welcome to them,' said Giles, smiling and looking round at the books, some of which were vertical and some horizontal, some stacked at odd angles, propped up against each other, and some upside down. It was a sad sight for Philip, the dishevelment and disregard of the emblems of learning and culture, but Giles was not as disturbed as he would have been had the books been sheep and one of them had been 'cast', as used to be said of a sheep that had fallen on its back and couldn't get up and would die unless rescue came—or had even been injured in a less serious way. Philip made no comment except to say, 'They seem to be nice books—at least they have nice bindings. Can I have a look at them?'

'Of course,' his friend said, 'I had forgotten you were a bookworm. Have a good feed on them, but don't forget to turn the light off when you go. I've got a little job to do with a sick animal, but it doesn't involve you.'

Left to himself, under the pale bulb that kept the granary in half darkness, Philip examined the books, the remains of a 'gentleman's library'. Half of the names he couldn't read, so poor was the light from above, but every now and then he made out a name or two, and then he saw on the floor, collapsing against each other like an inebriate pack of cards, a beautiful calf-bound series of volumes. Peering closer, he deciphered their title: Gibbon's *Decline and Fall of the Roman Empire*.

I have never read this, he thought, and I ought to have. A sudden feeling that literature, not agriculture, was his true occupation, came over him. 'What matter if I am potentially T.B.?' he asked himself; 'I can still read, as well as tend to the hindquarters of sheep.'

He took at random one of the eight volumes and opened it. The print and the paper delighted him. Could it be a first edition? No, not possibly. But what was this, this document, concealed between the pages? Something, he supposed, that belonged to the original owner of the book, for how many books changed hands!

'This is the last Will and testament of'—who was Giles's grandfather? It must be he; Philip took the book, and the document in it, and switched out the light as he had been asked to. In the hour that remained before dinner-time he studied the Will, which was in fact short enough. 'What difference will this Will make to them?' he asked himself. 'And how desirable is it to upset arrangements which have lasted, for good or ill, for so many years? To reverse so many things that have been accepted and taken for granted by a good many people? To dash many hopes and encourage others? To make a stroke of the pen demolish lives which—for how many years?—have been accepted on a certain basis of living?'

Philip wasn't late for dinner's roast lamb, but he had little to say to enliven the repast. 'Are you all right?' Hester asked him. 'Or are Jack and Giles being slave-drivers?' she asked rather anxiously, knowing how much, for them, depended on Philip's good-will. 'If so, you must tell them off. They are so sheep-minded they perhaps take you for one.'

Giles and his father exchanged smiles across the table.

'Oh no,' said Philip, trying to finish the lamb on his plate, 'I'm just a bit off colour, that's all.'

CHAPTER XIX

How hard it is to break bad news! And yet to break good news isn't always easy, when one doesn't know what its repercussions are going to be.

It was not a busy day on the farm and Jack and Giles, for obvious reasons, gave Philip all the time off that they could. If there was a lost sheep, they would look for it, not he.

Alone in his bedroom Philip studied the find he had made in the granary. The volume of Gibbon opened—it leapt to his eye, as such things often do—with the famous sentence that the major charge of heresy was withdrawn and that the Vicar of Christ was only accused of murder, rape, incest, piracy, etc.

His historical and already rather misanthropical view of human nature enjoyed this onslaught on the elected representative of Christianity in this world. Why try to be good when so many much more excellent persons, chosen to give religion a good name, were bad?

But the concerns of long ago were not his present concern. His present concern was Giles's grandfather's Will, duly signed and witnessed and now lying before him, a rather yellowing document —how old? Old, but young enough, as Philip could tell at a glance, to supersede the Will on which the testator's two daughters had inherited their money.

He couldn't remember the legal terms—with such reading they dissolved before his eyes—but the intention was plain. This Will revoked the testator's previous Wills and bequeathed all of what he was left possessed of to his younger daughter Hester. His elder daughter Judith, the Will said, was sufficiently provided for.

Of course, Philip had only one duty: to hand over the document to Jack and Hester. Yet still he hesitated; for how many people in the past had done good from which ill came? Here was the situation as he saw it:

Charlotte and Marcus were married. Whether they were happily married was no business of his—or was it? They had a baby boy—more than that Philip did not know, for Giles and Charlotte, so far as Philip knew, were scarcely on writing terms. Meanwhile Charlotte and Marcus, with his business prosperity, must be living the life of Riley in Havant, Hants; asked everywhere, giving continual parties, adored and courted and coveted by their neighbours, queening and kinging it over the social life of Havant.

Why upset this arrangement? On the other hand, here in Cumberland Hester and Jack lived a hard life, and how deeply, what a deep hole, Charlotte's desertion had made in Giles's nature he didn't know, and perhaps he was too young to know how people conceal the hurts that matter most to them. No partygiving (Giles hardly ever saw a girl, except a female sheep), no personal distractions, nothing to take them away from the kitchen, the sitting-room and the fells, where, like Norva's father on the Grampian hills, Jack kept his sheep, with the help of Giles and Philip, who were not always as assiduous as they should have been, especially Philip, who felt that as he contributed to making the farm a going concern he need do no unnecessary chores.

Giles and his father were away somewhere, striding over the fells; Philip, pleading a slight indisposition, he didn't say what, had asked to be excused. Hester, who really ruled the household, and dreaded losing him, at once said yes.

Released from his pastoral duties he at once returned to the Will.

Jack and Hester were quite resigned, so far as Philip could make out, to the unfairness of old Mr. Handforth's Will, and so he thought was Giles, of whose letter from his cousin, Charlotte, Philip knew nothing.

The Will and the Way

Why disturb these arrangements which Fate had decreed, and which its objects, or its victims, seemed to be content with? The pattern had unfolded itself; the people concerned had accepted it, as most people do when *force majeure* enforces it. People are not necessarily unhappy for long because they have lost money to which they were entitled; nor are they necessarily unhappy for long because they have lost what seemed to be the love of a lifetime.

Looking again at the Will, Philip wondered, 'Shall I suppress it? Shall I tear it up? Shall I leave things to take their course, as Fate seems to have intended?'

He heard voices at the door, loud, cheerful voices, Jack and Giles coming in from their adventures with the sheep.

'How are you?' said Jack. 'Better, I hope. You looked a bit off-colour this morning.'

'Oh, much better,' said Philip, 'quite well, in fact. But when you have a moment to spare—'

'My time is your time,' said Jack, taking off his furred cap which made him look like an Eskimo.

'There's something I want to tell you—not really important.'

'I'm thankful for that,' said Jack. 'No sheep trouble, I hope?'

'Oh no, nothing of that sort.'

'You're not getting tired of country life?' And Jack began to shake off his sheepskin jacket.

'Oh no, nothing of that sort.'

'Can it wait until after lunch?' Jack asked, who had noticed the change in Philip's manner.

'Oh yes, whenever you like.'

Hester was hovering round them, with a cook's anxiety on her face.

'Shall we drink to it? We've still got a drop of some South African sherry.'

'As you please,' said Philip, and his heart rose and then sank. 'As you please.'

CHAPTER XX

AFTER lunch Philip felt bolder, as well as more optimistic, about revealing the nature of his discovery. But still he didn't know how to put it into words; he couldn't foresee the family's reactions. Would it be a damp squib? At every minute more bewildered and embarrassed by what might, or might not be, the facts of the case, Philip looked round the familiar table where he had had so many plain but satisfying meals.

'Out with it,' said Jack, jovial and even jocular, as he sipped his brandy. 'Don't keep us in suspense.'

To gain time and to try to come to terms with his own feelings Philip said:

'I give you three guesses.'

At once their faces changed; he was the inquisitor, not they.

'Jack?'

Jack tried to think.

'Anything about the new tractor?'

Philip shook his head.

'How silly you are,' Hester interposed, 'to imagine it's got anything to do with us! So like a man who can't see any farther than his own yardstick. Tractor, indeed! I'm sure it's something to do with Phil. He's going to announce his engagement—that's what makes him look so shy, eh, Phil? Are we drinking to the health of your bride?' And even as she said the word, the beautiful word, the smile faded from her face.

Philip again shook his head, regaining confidence from their

The Will and the Way

mistakes. 'Wrong, wrong, Hester. If it had been, I would have told you, and anyhow you would have known.'

Hester looked at once relieved and disappointed, as if Philip's repudiation of his engagement had cast a slight on all the female sex.

Still in command of the situation Philip asked:

'What do you think, Giles?'

Giles, who had been preparing his answer, said:

'Has it anything to do with the granary?'

'The granary?' Jack asked.

'The granary?' echoed Hester. 'You mean that old barn that we never use?' Her voice sounded even more incredulous than Jack's.

'You're right,' said Philip, at last emerging from his shell of secrecy. 'It has to do with the granary.'

All the other faces round the table, including Giles's, fell.

'You've led us up the garden-path,' said Jack, impatiently. 'There's nothing in the granary to interest us, or you, I should think, Phil. I haven't been there myself for years. In fact I thought of pulling it down, we don't need it. There's nothing there except some old books—'

'Ah,' said Philip, 'but I found something in one of those old books.' The strain of concealment had become too great, and he brought out from under the chair the volume of Gibbon with its irreverent reference to the Pope, opened the page, and produced the document.

No one was interested.

Philip's squib couldn't have been damper.

'It may be of importance to scholars,' said Jack doubtfully, throwing his head back and straightening his shoulders, as though to rid them of the incubus of scholar's work, 'but it can't matter much to us.'

He didn't want, nor did anyone else at the table want to stretch out a hand to look at Philip's discovery and for a moment, piqued by their half-amused faces, he thought, with the document still under his hand, 'Why should I bother to show it them? As Jack says, "it might only be of interest to scholars".'

He closed the book and looked at Hester for a sign to rise. After a moment's pause, Jack and Giles got up and began to collect the plates; but Hester remained seated and, seeing that Philip was offended, said:

'Please tell us, Phil, what you have found.'

'Oh, I don't think it would interest you,' said Philip.

'But you said it had something to do with us.'

'It has,' said Philip, 'but I'm sure it's not important, and I think I'll keep it to myself.'

Giles and his father had come back into the room, with the anticipation of the afternoon's work already alight in their faces.

'Coming with us?' said Jack to Philip. 'Don't if you're still feeling off-colour.'

'Wait a moment,' Hester said, 'he wants to show us something.'

Impatiently the two farmers bent their heads over the table.

'Out with it!'

Philip conquered his irritation, opened the book and handed the document to Jack.

'This is the last Will and Testament—'

Jack sat down heavily on his chair, Giles followed his example, Hester and Philip remained respectfully seated, while Jack scrutinized his father-in-law's Will. It was very short, only a page to turn over.

He turned to Philip with a face so changed that Philip hardly recognized it—the bones stuck out so much and the shadows around them were so deep.

'Why didn't you show me this before?' he demanded.

'I only found it last night, and you didn't give me a chance,' retorted Philip.

'You've read it, I suppose?' said Jack.

'Yes, it was between the pages of the book and addressed to no one in particular.'

The Will and the Way

Jack sighed and the silence that followed seemed to contain the essence of half a lifetime.

'We must talk about this,' he said, handing the Will—so thin, a mere slip of paper—to Hester, 'and Giles, you must see it too. Perhaps I should see Greenwood' (Greenwood was their solicitor) 'this afternoon. There isn't much to be done on the farm, Phil, but would you just have a look round?'

There was a new note of respect, and perhaps of apology, in his voice. 'Of course, Mr. Holroyd.'

*

When the conclave was over, and Jack had made an appointment with his solicitor for later in the afternoon, he said:

'God knows what difference this is going to make to us.'

'Or to them,' said his wife, meaning her sister Judith, and Charlotte and Marcus and their child.

'I don't think it will make all that difference. The Will leaves all that your father died possessed of to you; and it adds "I understand that my daughter Judith is sufficiently provided for." '

'I suppose she is,' said Hester. 'We don't know, we haven't been in touch with them.'

'The merger was going to make Seymour a packet—'

'Well, perhaps it has.'

'Do you think your Dad knew about it when he made this Will?'

'I wonder,' Hester said.

'He must have known *something*, to leave the whole of his estate to you. We don't know how much that was,' said Jack. 'It may be something, it may be nothing.' He looked at Giles, whose face had become as puzzled as his own. 'Well, don't let's feel too hopeful or too doubtful, but let's go into Carlisle and hear what Greenwood has to say.'

CHAPTER XXI

'IT MAY mean a law-suit,' said Jack, when they came home and their bedroom doors were closed. Giles was in his, and Philip was presumably in his. 'But Greenwood evidently thinks we have a right to the money.'

'Fifty thousand pounds, he said.'

'Yes, your Dad was quite well-off. Greenwood said they'll have to fork out, supposing they can and haven't spent what your father left to Judith.'

'Yes, ours was a pittance. The winner—that was Judith—takes all.'

He didn't disguise the triumph in his voice. 'And now, according to Greenwood, it will come to us.'

'It's going to cause a lot of unpleasantness,' said Hester.

'Yes, but you can't make an omelette without breaking eggs. It caused some unpleasantness to us when your father left most of his money to Judith.'

'Yes, but he didn't leave it all.'

'Enough for them to live a gay life in Havant while we were starving, with the help of our lodger, on the Cumberland fells.'

'If we get this money, *if* we get this money, what will Philip do?'

'He'll come in with us, I hope,' said Jack. 'We shall be able to offer him more than we can now. He's a good, useful lad, he works for the sake of working—and we shan't charge him anything. We might even pay him something!'

Jack laughed, the first laugh he had made as solvent, or as prospectively solvent, for many years.

The Will and the Way

'And Charlotte,' asked Hester, who couldn't share her husband's optimism, his reaction from the long anxiety of straitened circumstances, 'how will she feel, if she isn't any more the social queen of Havant?'

Jack chuckled heartlessly.

'She will be the vice-reine of Havant, I suppose. Not vice in the nasty sense. She's had a good time, and can afford to play second fiddle.'

He laughed again.

But blood is thicker than water, and little as Hester had to be grateful to her sister for, she foresaw the commotion that was certain to ensue.

'Are we all right as we are?'

'We should be better off with £50,000.'

'Was Greenwood positive that we should get it?'

'Yes. He said it may take some time—all lawyer's work does. If we farmers kept our customers waiting as long as they do, we should soon be on the rocks.'

'And it depends on whether they can pay up or not?'

'Of course they can. They must have pots of money. Fifty thousand pounds will be a mere flea-bite to them—not half of what Charlotte married Marcus for. And then they had the advantage of your father's money—you and I could only just subsist on our small share, but they must have made packets out of theirs, what with the merger and all.'

Jack was not a resentful man; so many factors in his life, not owing to any effort of his own, had prevented that. It was about the first time that Hester had heard resentment in his voice.

For some reason, Hester couldn't quite share the enormous elation that her father's long-lost Will had brought to Jack. He saw it as a refuge from chronic imminent insolvency; she, less fortunate, and knowing the scarcity of domestic help in the district, did not immediately envisage the same release from chronic household drudgery. He, through rose-coloured spectacles, saw the figures in his bank-account change from red to black; she, less sanguine, wondered if she could now persuade Mrs. Helpwhite to come for a couple of hours in the morning.

'What do you think Giles will feel about this?'

'Giles?' repeated Jack, whose mind was far away.

'Yes, Giles. After all, he was Charlotte's boy-friend, and still more was she his, until she got married.'

'Oh, I think he's got over it,' said Jack, stretching himself and now looking larger than life, as though these years of financial stringency had somehow diminished him. 'I think he's got over it. Why shouldn't he? They haven't seen each other for I don't know how many years. I don't think Giles has any more feelings for Charlotte—why should he have, when she threw him over for Marcus and his money? Perhaps he'll find someone else now; he hasn't had much chance, slaving away on the hillside, with nothing to offer to any girl. The sort of girls that Giles meets—and I don't think he meets many—want much more lucre than Giles could give them.'

'Are you sure of that? Are they all so mercenary?'

'Well, we are told so.'

Hester thought for a while. The electric lights shone brightly and securely, not as if they might at any moment be cut off; the whole house seemed to settle itself comfortably into its foundations, as if at last it had found something capable of taking care of it.

'What a difference it will make to us,' murmured Jack, still far away in his dream of affluence.

'What shall we do first?'

'Well, perhaps put in central heating,' said Hester, following her own thoughts.

'Well, that's a good idea, but I was thinking more of the farm, and what we should do there.'

'You remember that Greenwood said they might contest the Will and that anyhow it would take a long time before we got the money.'

The Will and the Way

'Yes, but he said we *should* get it. I shall go to the Bank tomorrow and tell them.'

Nothing could disturb Jack's optimism; it was the measure of his release from the pessimism he had fought against for so long.

CHAPTER XXII

NOTHING happened, of course, for two or three weeks, and then Hester got a letter from her sister Judith:

'My darling Hester,
   We haven't written to each other for some time, which I much regret, but I expect you have been as busy as I have—though not quite for the same urgent reason. Two grandchildren—a girl and a boy. Charlotte is so delighted with them, and so is Seymour, and so of course is Marcus, their proud father. I wish that you could see them. But alas, you live so far away! And you couldn't come to either of the christenings—I can quite understand that, but you would have met so many old friends, besides your devoted Judith.
   The children take up a good deal of my time, as well as Charlotte's—I have become an expert baby-sitter, and when Charlotte is out on one of the many commitments she has—hospital work, committees of various sorts, mostly to do with schools (she has become quite an authority on education, believe it or not!) and social occasions, which she goes to as little as she can help—well, then I have to stand in for her. There are still uses for a grandmother!
   Forgive me, dearest, this long preamble, but it is just to put you into the picture of how things are here. Life is a bit of a strain, as you know as well as I do.
   Well, I've just heard from your solicitors the strange news that Daddy, before he died, made another Will, in which he left everything he had to you! I'm sure it was his intention to leave us

both equal shares, but for some reason, I can't imagine what, he seems to have changed his mind! I know that as it turned out, I got more than you did, but that was because his house, our old house, turned out to be more valuable than he thought, and his stocks and shares less. The house and garden were in the middle of the town and their value rocketed up; but according to this last Will, which the solicitors say is authentic, he left you everything he had, including the shares, which didn't amount to very much, and altogether it comes to quite a large sum.

I can't imagine why he did this, for we were always on the best of terms, and I can only think that after his stroke he wasn't quite himself. But the Will seems to be legal and how we shall find the money, goodness knows!

I expect you and Jack are just as busy as Seymour and I are. You probably can't spare the time to come down south, and we should find it difficult to get away at this moment (even if you had room for us—no insult intended!—but no one knows more about shortage of space and domestic difficulties than I do). Although we are geographically separated by 250 miles and more, as a family we have always been very close—and it has been a great grief to me that during these last years we have seen so little of each other, and I wondered if, supposing it were possible, Giles would come down here and pay us a visit—I believe you have an apprentice (lucky you!) who could stand in for him for a few days. We should all love to see him, and Charlotte would rejoice to renew their childhood friendship. They were so fond of each other, do you remember, and I once used to hope—but it was not to be.

Marcus is out most of the day, and sometimes spends the night at Bristol, where he has business interests, which alas are not doing very well. But if he and Giles could get together, with Charlotte, who has quite a good head for business, making a third, they might be able to work out something to our mutual advantage, and if they can't, we shall have had the pleasure of seeing Giles, who must be quite a man now (twenty-four, twenty-five?)—six months older than Charlotte, who was so devoted to him. I could find out if she would lend me her birthday-book, in which his name I believe was the *first* entry, how many years ago!

With all my love, darling, and I hope we shall be able to make this partial—but not impartial! (if you get me)—family reunion.

Judith.'

Hester's first reaction to this letter was anger. Every word, she thought, is a lie, or an implied lie; they deliberately cut themselves off from us because we were not in their income bracket. Judith knew—she must have known—that Charlotte wanted to marry Giles, but supposing he had had the temerity to propose it, which his mother did not know, for Giles was naturally secretive, she had demolished his feeble lead with her ace, Marcus.

And now that Marcus was apparently, apparently, not doing too well, she hoped that Charlotte would somehow get round Giles—for she knew enough about him to know he was not married—to make a compromise with her father's second Will.

What impudence! Never!

Had she known of Charlotte's proposal to Giles to make a more than shadowy third in their matrimonial arrangements, she would have been even more indignant than she was. But there was enough in her sister's letter to show that Giles would receive a warm welcome from Charlotte.

Hester's first instinct was not to answer the letter. For years they had not corresponded, and now, because Judith saw a red light ahead, she had written. To hell with her! Let the law take its course.

She showed the letter to Jack, and when he, being an unsuspicious character, took it at its face value, and was even rather touched by it, she pointed out the trap and falsehoods which underlay it.

He, still intoxicated by the thought of their coming fortune, was unwilling to be convinced.

'Do you mean that Judith might work on Giles to make him give up our claim on your father's estate?'

The Will and the Way

'No, I don't think she would, but I think Charlotte might. She was very thick with Giles before she threw him over, persuaded by her mother, to marry this wealthy Marcus, whom she pretends —but who knows?—is not so well off now.'

Jack tried to adjust his mind from money—legal money, signed, sealed and witnessed in his wife's favour—to the emotional influences which might affect it to their detriment.

'But she hasn't seen the boy for years,' he said. 'She's married and according to Judith she has two children; why should she be interested in Giles—or he in her? He never looks at a girl, as far as I know. Rather odd, but so it is.'

'Couldn't it be that he still remembers Charlotte, and that Charlotte remembers him?'

Jack didn't distrust his wife's judgement but he had been for so long wrapped up in the the farm and its fluctuating fortunes that he didn't quite see how it could be affected by her far-away relations in Havant.

'I can't see what harm it would do if the boy went down to see them,' Jack said. 'He hasn't seen them for ages. Phil and I can look after the farm while he is away. It might be a bit embarrassing for him, but more embarrassing for them, I should have thought. After all, we have the law on our side.'

Hester looked at him, and her old affection for him shone in her eyes.

'You may be a good farmer,' she said, 'and a good businessman—though I'm not so sure of that. But you don't understand women's wiles.'

Jack sat up, almost affronted, in the easy chair, which he seldom occupied, opposite the log-wood fire playing on his face.

'Do you mean I don't *understand* women? I'm a married man, I've been through what most men have.'

'Yes, I'm sure that's true, but I don't think you do.'

There was silence for a minute or two, and Hester watched the fire playing on his face, its hills and hollows.

'You may be right,' he said. 'Do you think we should show

Giles Judith's letter or tell him what's in it? Or if we do show it to him, should we advise him not to go?'

Hester looked round the firelit room, moderately warm where they were sitting, but bitterly cold at its extremities. How comfortable it would be with central-heating!

'I don't know,' she said. 'I think we ought to show Giles the letter, on what might be moral grounds. After all it concerns him, and the money may come to him before it comes to us, if I know anything about lawyers' methods. But I think we ought to warn him—'

'Yes?'

'Not to commit himself in any way, in any way whatsoever, to Judith or Charlotte, that blest pair of sirens.'

Jack didn't know the reference, but he said, 'You think they might try to prevail on his good nature—for he's a dear boy, isn't he?'

'Yes, very dear.'

'To divide the money with them.'

'Or take it all,' said Hester tartly.

Jack tried to recall the passage of the years since Charlotte's wedding, which they had refused to attend. Giles hadn't got married, it was true—a big fine fellow like him—nor seemed to want to get married. Jack had been too busy with the sheep to speculate much about his son's love-life, if any. A feeling of guilt pierced him. After all, whatever may be said about it nowadays, some parents have a sense of responsibility towards their offspring.

'Do you think he was really attached to Charlotte, and that's why he doesn't seem interested in women?'

'I think she was really more interested in him,' said Hester, 'and that may have put him off. "Around his neck the albatross—"' She didn't continue the quotation, for Jack clearly didn't recognize it—'but I've no doubt that he hasn't forgotten her, or she him.'

'Um,' said Jack.

'I think there's a risk if he goes down there,' went on Hester. 'After all, we owe them nothing, less than nothing. They've always treated us as poor relations. Now they are frightened, possibly, though I doubt it—I think that Giles is a "soft touch", as they say, and if they, or if Charlotte, can get round him, it will save them several thousands.'

Jack was impressed by all this, and the possibility of his father-in-law's legacy passing into alien hands.

'So your advice is not to let him go there? I can easily say sorry, we can't spare him from the farm.'

'It would be the safest thing to do,' said Hester. 'He's so impressionable and he finds it so hard to say no. All the same—' she added, and stopped.

'Yes?'

'If he was warned, thoroughly warned, and put on his guard as to what they were up to, it might be interesting to know what their reactions were. If we could rely on him to stand firm and say we are not prepared to give away a pound of the money that Daddy left us—well, I should be quite interested to know how they behave.'

'They?'

'Well, all of them, especially Charlotte.'

Suddenly Jack, as a man who had a man's experience, looked at it all more objectively than Hester, with her romantic feminine notions, had. Giles would be put on the spot. They would appeal to his compassion, tell him how hard up they were; Charlotte (he had an intuitive prevision of this) might even cry on his shoulder. She might even ask him, when Marcus was conveniently away in Bristol, to—

'We must tell Giles, of course,' he said, 'and ask him what he would like to do. But I have another idea. Why not ask Phil to go down to Havant and spy out the land? He could be our envoy; he has no connections with the family; and he wouldn't be subject to the pressure they might try to bring on Giles.'

'It is an idea,' said Hester, with her eye on the kitchen door. 'It is an idea. They might even go together, backing each other up.'

CHAPTER XXIII

'IF I were you,' said Philip a day or two later, 'I should let the law take its course. I shouldn't dream of going down to Havant, or whatever it's called. It's quite plain from your Aunt's letter' (Giles had told him of Judith's letter) 'that they'll try to get round you, and work on your family feeling, if you have any—'

'As a matter of fact I have,' said Giles, and his face took on an expression that Philip had never seen there before; it was not the almost affectionate, certainly solicitous look that Giles turned on the sheep's faces, and even on their rumps. 'I have a family feeling, but not a very friendly one. I could probably have been married long ago if—'

'If your cousin Charlotte hadn't thrown you over?'

'Yes, for that and other things. Her mother cheated us out of a lot of money.' His face changed and softened. 'If it hadn't been for that, and being always in the red, or near it, you and I wouldn't be the friends we are. You have kept us afloat.'

Philip was silent for a moment. Then he said, 'Well, as far as I'm concerned, your aunt did a good deed.'

'Thank you,' said Giles, 'but don't think that all these years of privation that my parents have had to suffer—comparative privation, of course—thanks to you, we've kept our heads above water—but we haven't had a holiday for I don't know how long—don't you think my well-to-do relations should suffer for this?'

'But they will, Giles, if they have to fork out all this money.'

'Yes, if they do. But sometimes I think I should like to rub it in.'

'How?'

The Will and the Way

'By telling them what I think, and especially by telling Charlotte what I think. She married this rich chap Marcus and left me high and dry, with nothing to look at, or to love, but sheep. One, two, three, four, good-night darling, five, six, seven—I must admit I've grown quite fond of them.'

Philip wondered how seriously Giles was taking this.

'I still think,' he said, 'you would do better to refuse your aunt's invitation, making the excuse that you are too busy to get away—and their lawyers must settle it between them. That's what I should do—it will be punishment enough to know what's hanging over them. £50,000, did you say? It's a tidy sum and may give them many a sleepless night, unless they are as rich as you say.'

'I should guess they are much richer,' said Giles, and the new, unfamiliar accent rasped in his voice. 'But what I should like, Phil, is a *personal* revenge.'

'On whom?' asked Philip.

'On Aunt Judith and her daughter'—he hesitated for the name—'her daughter Charlotte. They didn't care a damn what happened to us. We might have been in the bankruptcy court—or worse, in jug—for all they cared. No, I think they should be punished.'

'How?'

'Through Charlotte, perhaps. She is their most vulnerable point.'

Philip gave a slight shiver.

'But wasn't she in love with you?'

'Yes, so she always said, and she still may be.' He took a long breath and told his friend and confidant the proposal Charlotte had made to him after her marriage, that Giles and she should become what they had never been before, lovers.

'Did you answer this letter?' Philip asked.

'No, but I could act on it now, or someone could act on it for me.'

Philip raised his eyebrows.

'Who, for instance?'

'Well, I mention no names. No names, no pack-drill.'

Philip laughed.

'Are you suggesting that I should try to seduce your cousin, that is, if you can technically seduce a married woman?'

'One can but try,' said Giles. 'She's quite attractive, or she used to be. And her mother has emphasized the point that she will have a good deal of time on her hands, while Marcus is on business in Bristol—what business, she doesn't say.'

'Then why not do your own dirty work?' asked Philip.

Giles, the new Giles, a Giles who was unknown to Philip, and perhaps unknown to Giles himself, replied:

'Oh well, I don't want to see her, really.'

'And have you been bottling it up all this time?'

'Bottling what up?'

'Your grievance against your cousin and her mother.'

Giles hesitated, and the new Giles looked out of his eyes.

'Perhaps I have,' he said, 'perhaps I have. You see, my Aunt Judith, working on Grandad's feelings, ruined—well, ruined is an exaggeration—but she kept us nearer to the bread line, and she kept Charlotte and me from getting married, which we both should have liked.'

'Charlotte as much as you?'

'Yes, more, I think.'

'And you resented that?'

'Yes, I never wanted to marry anyone else. Partly from disillusion, I suppose. I got used to it, a flock of sheep is worth Charlotte's ransom.'

He laughed bitterly.

How little one knows, thought Philip, about one's closest friends! Here is Giles, the shepherd, loving his sheep so much and so contented in their company that he has almost grown to look like one—a ram perhaps, lean and spare, he might be, for Giles in his present mood, with his elbows on the table and his eyes turning inwards and outwards, and alight with hostility, didn't look very sheep-like and I should never have guessed what thoughts he was harbouring.

'And you blame Charlotte?' he asked.

'I do. She said she loved me and wanted to marry me—she said it more than once.'

'And do you think she is unhappy with her Marcus?'

'I've no idea, but her mother's letter suggests she is at liberty.'

'At liberty for what?'

Giles shrugged his shoulders.

'At liberty to make me, or anyone, take a more lenient view of Grandad's second Will. For a consideration, of course.'

'What consideration?'

'Need you ask?'

Philip was silent for a moment, then:

'What a strange fellow you are,' he said. 'Have you any reason, apart from your aunt's letter, which only says that Marcus is sometimes away from home, to think she would be open to an offer of that kind?'

'Yes, I have,' said Giles vehemently.

'But how do I come in?'

'You would be there to hold my hand.'

'But you would be holding *her* hand.'

'Not necessarily. *You* might be holding it.'

'Goodness,' cried Philip, 'are you a pander?'

'Well, not a giant panda,' replied Giles, with a flash of humour that was as foreign to his old self as to his present self, 'just a pigmy one.' He closed his eyes and seemed to collapse into himself.

'You are quite right, Phil. Better not go there at all. Let them stew in their own juice, or frizzle in their lack of it—which I doubt.'

But Philip's curiosity had been aroused and with it a realization of how much his friend had suffered in pocket, pride and personal emotion since the time his cousin had married Marcus.

'Of course I'll go with you, Giles,' he said warmly, 'if you think I could be of any help, vengeance-wise or any other wise.' He already foresaw what might be coming and made up his mind quickly, as he had when answering the Holroyd's advertisement for a farmer's apprentice. 'But I think I had better stay in a hotel in Havant, don't you? rather than in your aunt's house, or in Charlotte's, supposing they could have me? Then I should be independent and at the same time be at your beck and call, supposing you have need of me, which I doubt. Your father could dispense with us for two or three days—the sheep aren't lambing or doing anything sexually serious.'

Giles suddenly looked much older, and as if his whole future was at stake.

'It's very kind of you, Phil, and I should feel much more comfortable if you were within hail. I would like some sort of explanation, not so much from Aunt Judith, who would have all her answers ready as to why they behaved as they did, but from Charlotte. And they couldn't pull the wool over your eyes as they could over mine.'

Philip laughed at the metaphor.

'Are you still under Charlotte's spell?' he asked. 'Or do you want me to fall for it, or seem to fall for it?'

Giles drew a deep breath—several deep breaths—before he answered.

'I can't tell you that, Phil, before I see her. Nobody knows—at least in my experience, which isn't much—what they will feel in the future. Even sheep don't know—lucky for them!'

'But you don't mean to give way about the Will?' asked Philip. 'You don't mean to make the smallest concession?'

'No,' said Giles, and his mobile features stiffened. 'That's partly why I want to go there. I want to see them *squirm*.'

CHAPTER XXIV

THE door opened on to what, in a provincial town, was almost a stately house. It was opened, however, by Judith herself, who flung her arms round Giles, kissed him on both cheeks and exclaimed.

'Welcome, my long-lost nephew!' Giles, disengaging himself as well as he could, turned round to Philip, at his rear, and said:

'This is my friend Philip Oakeshott, who helps us on the farm.'

Judith, taken aback, shook hands with Philip.

'He's my travelling companion,' explained Giles, 'and my co-shepherd.'

He smiled as his aunt's face fell.

'He wanted to see you,' went on Giles, as naturally as he could, 'he's heard so much about you. And also he wanted to see Havant, so he's booked a room at the Royal Hotel.'

Judith's face brightened.

'The Royal is very good, I'm always told,' she said, as if the nature of a hotel in Havant was unfamiliar to her, 'and I hope you will be very comfortable there, Mr. . . . Mr. . . .'

'Oakeshott,' said Philip, wishing for some reason that he had another name.

'I wish I could have asked you to stay here,' said Aunt Judith, insincerely. 'We have a cook, a dear old thing who has been with us for years, but like so many other people, we have domestic difficulties. Our housemaid, if you can call her one, is temperamental, and this evening she has taken herself off, which is why I had to open the door for you. But come in, come in.' And she led them into the brightly-lit hall with its white walls and nice eighteenth-century furniture. 'I feel so inhospitable,' she said, turning to Philip, 'not to be able to ask you to stay. But at any rate, you will dine with us, won't you, and come for any meal that doesn't interfere with your plans for exploring Havant. People make fun of the name—but it really has quite a lot to show. Now I'm sure you must be tired after your long journey and be longing for a drink—unless you would rather have a wash first? If so, it's on the left, and then straight on.'

Giles and Philip availed themselves of her invitation, and when they came back found her waiting for them in the hall.

'Now for the drinks,' she said. 'They're in my husband's study —at least they ought to be.'

She led the way and there indeed they were, a panoply of drinks set on a glass-topped table under a mirror, which reflected a huge writing-desk and other opulent furnishings of the well-to-do business man.

'Please choose for yourselves,' said their hostess, 'I myself shall have a little tonic water, which is all my doctor allows me.' She sighed. 'Seymour will be here in a few minutes. Nowadays he often has to stay late at the office—times are hard, as I expect you know, Giles.'

Giles agreed, and he and Philip raised their glasses to her.

'Sometimes I think the strain on him is too great for a man of his years; not that he's really old, but he often looks tired. Now in Cumberland—'

'In Cumberland?' repeated Giles.

'Life must be very different, much more healthy, as I can see by looking at your faces. The open-air life, the freedom of the hills, and the absence of *worry*—'

'But we do have our worries,' Giles said. 'Don't we, Phil?'

Philip agreed. 'Yes, it isn't all beer and skittles, Mrs. Snape. Especially when there's snow on the hills, and we have to dig the sheep out.'

'Oh yes, how terrible that must be. But it all makes for health, doesn't it? And health is our most precious possession, worth its weight in gold.'

She listened to the closing of the door. 'That must be Seymour. He'll be with us in a few minutes. We never change—except for special occasions—but he always likes to tidy himself up for dinner. Charlotte is coming too—she's so excited by the thought of meeting you, Giles, she may even have put on a long dress—which I haven't, I'm ashamed to say, being acting house maid. Marcus, alas, is in Bristol on business; he hates it, poor boy, but what can one do? He'll be with us tomorrow, or the next day. Of course he's longing to see you, Giles, but needs must, when the devil drives! Don't you think so, Mr. Oakeshott?'

'Well,' said Philip, 'Giles may be a devil, but he doesn't drive me.'

'Oh, how lucky you are. Here it is a rat-race, everyone treading on each other's heels, and devil take the hindmost. Speak of the devil—'

At that moment the door opened and Mr. Snape, spruce and elegant in a dark suit, appeared.

'Why, there's Giles!' he exclaimed, coming forward to shake his hand. 'Giles, after all these years! I should have known you anywhere, Giles, you're the spitting image of your father, the best-looking man I ever saw. I can't say more than that. Will Charlotte recognize him, Judith, or shall we have to introduce him?'

'I shall have to introduce you to Mr. Oakeshott,' said Judith, rising as Philip rose. 'He's a friend of Giles, and therefore a friend of ours—they are partners, lucky fellows, in an agricultural estate in Cumberland.'

'Delighted to meet you,' said Seymour, warmly shaking hands with this unexpected guest.

When the genial noises of introduction were over, Giles said rather coldly, 'We're only sheep-farmers really.'

'Oh,' said his aunt, 'I'm sorry if I mis-described you—Hester often asked us to stay at Helvellyn Farm but, alas, we've never been able to go.'

Giles knew this to be a lie, a double lie, but to someone who has no temperamental inclination for it rudeness doesn't come easily; besides, he had to think of Philip, who wouldn't want to be embroiled in family disagreements, so he contented himself with saying:

'It's a pretty place, a bit bare, you know—for the sheep, I mean—but very good for walking. We do a lot of walking, don't we, Phil?—looking for lost sheep.'

'It sounds an ideal existence,' said Aunt Judith. 'Wordsworth adored it and so did all the Lake poets... Now where is Charlotte? She's always late, the naughty child.'

There was a sound of footsteps in the hall. 'Ah, perhaps that's she.' But silence followed. 'It must be Elsie coming in from her afternoon out. But it means we shall get some dinner. You must be desperately hungry,' said Aunt Judith, turning to Philip. 'We'll give Charlotte a little longer.'

The conversation straggled on in a desultory way, as conversations do when awaiting a late arrival, and then, without warning, the door opened and Charlotte appeared.

'I'm so sorry,' she began.

'We've heard that before,' her father said. 'Now this is Mr. Oakeshott, a friend of Giles, and the rest of us you know. Now, you have just time for a drink.'

Charlotte shook hands with Philip on her way to the drink table, but her eyes were on Giles, as his were on her.

Each was struck by the other's maturity; they had still been teenagers when they last saw each other. There was a lean, a weatherbeaten look about Giles, making him look older than his years, which surprised and pleased her; she, to him, also looked older than her age, and more sophisticated, as if she had rubbed on to, and into, her face the artificial colours of a long experience —so changed from the schoolgirl he had known. This didn't please him. She was wearing a long dress and had obviously taken pains with her appearance. She didn't look like any of the women he knew, or wanted to know, in his district; she was a being from another sphere.

The Will and the Way

Mixing herself a drink she raised her glass to him.

'Here's to our reunion!'

'Here's to our disunion,' he thought, raising his to her.

'But Mr. Oakeshott hasn't got a drink,' she said, turning to Philip (how clever of her to remember his name!), 'Let me fill up your glass. What was it?'

He told her, and with careful but practised hands she mixed the cocktail for him. Their eyes met, with a warmer gleam in his than there had been in Giles's.

'Dinner is served,' said a voice in the doorway. The announcement was as unknown to Giles as the figure who uttered it; it was not unknown to Philip, but in his years of apprenticeship with the Holroyd's he had forgotten what it sounded like, or what a rare bird like Elsie looked like.

'We are five,' said Judith, rising to conduct them into the dining-room. 'Marcus wanted so much to be here but, as I told you, he's detained in Bristol. Business calls, but it doesn't always answer!' she added, on a mock-tragic note. 'Mr. Oakeshott, will you sit on my right, and the rest of us must sort ourselves out. Perhaps you, Seymour, would sit next to Mr. Oakeshott, and then Charlotte, and Giles must content himself with me—we can't divide the family—but I haven't seen him for so long that he's almost a stranger, and we shall have a lot to tell each other, shan't we, Giles?'

Giles, with his formidable aunt on one side and his hardly less formidable cousin on the other, felt at a loss; he had hardly ever been at a formal dinner-party, even so small as this, when they were being waited on by a straight-faced maid; for at home they always waited on themselves, jumping up from the table to satisfy their wants. Confined to his chair, he had a feeling of claustrophobia which increased his resentment. Why did I ever come? Philip was much more at his ease. He had no responsibility for the undeclared warfare at the table. Giles was accustomed to family relationships, in which one didn't talk from meal's end to meal's end if one didn't feel inclined to, or to business dealings concerning the price of sheep; warily worded and with no sense of sociability behind them, except a rather false *bonhomie*, he didn't know how to conduct himself in this polite society: he didn't know how to make conversation, but he knew that money-wise he had the upper hand, and that they daren't try to make him look a fool.

'Well, Giles,' said Charlotte, giving him a beaming look (her mother was occupied with Philip), 'it's so long since we saw each other. Much too long. Have you ever thought about me?'

'Oh yes,' said Giles, 'often.'

'I hope you thought about me kindly?'

Giles hated to tell a direct lie.

'I often think of those days,' he said, 'when we used to see so much of each other. They were—they were—great fun.' He felt rather proud of having achieved this phrase.

'I wrote you a letter,' said Charlotte. 'Do you remember? Perhaps you have forgotten. But you didn't answer it. Perhaps you have forgotten.'

Encouraged by the sound of voices round him, Giles said, 'No, I haven't forgotten. But should we talk about it another time?'

Giles waited while the next course was approaching, in case he should make some social blunder.

Having survived the ordeal, he said, with his mouth full:

'I couldn't agree to it, Charlotte.' He couldn't believe that such private and intimate matters could be discussed at a dinner-table.

'Why not?'

'Oh, for several reasons.' He looked round the table for help, but no help came. His aunt was busy carrying on a three-cornered conversation with Philip and her husband.

'You see, I live such a different life now.'

'You mean you don't care for me?'

'I don't mean that.'

'What do you mean?' and she flashed a look at him.

In a moment the social fabric between them crumbled.

'It's to do with Grandad's Will.'

'For God's sake,' cried Charlotte, in a voice that shattered the conversation like a scream, 'you're not going to bring that up at this time of day? Grandad was nuts when he made it, if he did make it. And have you no feeling for me any more?'

'Dear Giles,' said Aunt Judith, turning to him, 'we haven't had a word. Let's hand Charlotte over to her father. She's so busy with domestic and social chores, poor girl, she doesn't see him as often as she would like to, or Marcus either. He's kept so busy with his nose to the grindstone, trying to make both ends meet, otherwise, as I said, he would have been with us tonight. Such a pity! How lucky you are to be in agriculture, where things are so much more stable than they are here. You must be in clover!' She laughed. 'Do sheep eat clover?'

'Well, they will eat it,' conceded Giles, 'But they aren't mad about it. Anyhow, there isn't much of it where we live, we're too high up.'

'Too high for what?'

'Too high to be in clover,' said Giles, trying to get a bit of his own back.

CHAPTER XXV

'WELL, what did you think of it, Phil?' asked Giles, when they met next morning in the bar of the Royal Hotel.

'I was impressed, of course; I haven't had a meal like that for a long time. Not that I don't enjoy our meals at Helvellyn Farm better,' he added hastily. 'We always have the best mutton, and theirs wasn't.'

They ordered some drinks and while they were coming Giles said:

'I didn't enjoy it very much, all that display of wealth and pretence of poverty. Did you hear what Aunt Judith said?—when she was talking to me, I mean.'

'I caught a word here and there. She laid herself out to be nice to you, as was quite right.'

'Did she make out that they were paupers?'

'She said something about the fall of shares on the Stock Exchange had hit them hard.'

'I bet she did. And how lucky we sheep-farmers are?'

'Yes, she said something about that, too. It's the burden of the song.'

'And what did you say?'

'I laid it on quite thick. I said we were out from dawn to dusk, footsore and weary, rounding up the sheep.'

'Good boy.' At this moment the drinks arrived, paid for by Philip, and the two friends became more communicative with each other.

'And did you have any conversation with Seymour, my uncle?'

'Oh yes, when you stopped talking to your cousin Charlotte, we started a sort of three-cornered chat, mostly about business. I didn't let on, of course, that I knew how the land lay—I just sympathized with them about things in general. They wanted to know why I had taken to farming, and I said I was a friend of yours, and my health wasn't too good, and my doctor advised me to lead an open-air life. "How lucky you are to be able to afford it," your aunt said, and I replied, "Health comes before everything," or words to that effect. And I did say—I hope you don't mind, Giles—that my work on the farm was a small help to you as well as a great help to me.'

'Good boy, good boy,' repeated Giles, looking at Philip, whose dark-browned, handsome face was radiant with health, 'that would give them something to think about. Shall we have another drink?' he asked. 'Only this time they must be on me.'

While they were waiting, Giles said, 'You didn't mention my grandfather's Will?'

'Good Lord, no, you never asked me to, and in any case it's no business of mine.'

'Did they get the idea that you are fairly well off? Excuse me asking, but it means so much to them.'

'Not from anything I said,' replied Philip. 'I tried to give them the impression I wanted to be a dyed-in-the-wool farmer, as indeed I want to be, with no outside assets, except to pay you for my apprenticeship.'

'Did they seem disappointed?'

'If they did, they were too well-mannered to show it.'

'You haven't told me,' said Giles—the second round of drinks arrived, and they lifted their glasses—'what you thought of Charlotte.'

'Oh, Charlotte,' said Philip, a little vaguely. 'Yes, I did have a chat with her after dinner.'

'And what did you think of her?'

'Quite attractive. She is devoted to you, of course, and didn't hesitate to say so.'

'Did you say I was devoted to her?'

'I professed to know nothing about it. I explained that I had come down here to keep you company, because you hadn't had a holiday for a great many years and you didn't know how to look after yourself; I was your *homme de compagnie*, and fetched and carried for you.'

Giles smiled.

'What did she say to that?'

'She laughed and said she didn't remember you being so helpless. I said you weren't at all helpless where sheep were concerned, and if you were an animal and could take part in a sheep-dog trial, you would certainly win it. "He begins to look rather like an animal," she said, "that lean and hungry look." "Oh yes," I said, "but that's just the result of hard work, and being out in all weathers. He's a bit fine-drawn, as they say; he did two men's work before I came on the scene, and he still does the work of a man and a half. I take on some of the donkey-work, but all the responsibility rests on him and his father." '

'What a wonderful verbal memory you have,' said Giles admiringly. 'I can't remember what anyone says to me, unless—unless—'

'Unless what?'

'Unless it affects me, personally, very closely. Did she say anything else?'

'Only that you look a bit emaciated, if I may say so without offence. And she said, "It suits him to look a bit skinny. Most of us here—and I don't except myself—look as if we had done ourselves well. Our money has gone into our bodies and our clothes, and there it has stayed—at least, there it did stay, until it began to evaporate, as it is doing now. How lucky Giles is, and how lucky you are, to have no financial worries. You have only the sheep, which in turn will keep you." '

'Good God!' said Giles, astonished and indignant.

'And she said again how glad she was to see you, and how lonely she was with Marcus so much away, and the children were

The Will and the Way

a bind—I thing she finds them more of a nuisance than an interest.'

Thinking over what Philip had said, Giles didn't feel sorry for his aunt and her problems, and still less for Charlotte and hers.

'She could have married me, if she'd wanted to,' he said. 'She asked me often enough to marry her.'

'I know,' said Philip, 'but she was only a child then, and I suppose that circumstances alter cases.'

For the first time Giles felt annoyed with his old friend.

'She was quite old enough,' he said, 'to know her own mind. No, she chucked me because her mother persuaded her, if indeed she did persuade her, to marry Marcus for his money.'

'I think she's still in love with you,' Philip said.

'So she may be, so she may be, and I was in love with her long enough not to want to marry anyone else. Have you ever really been in love, Phil?'

'Oh yes, more than once.'

'That's it, love is a disease like 'flu, that can take some people many times, or it may be like mumps, something that you can only get once. It has been like mumps with me—'

'Well, now the tables have been turned. You must have noticed the efforts they have made—I don't know how they live in the ordinary way—to impress us with their wealth, by food of mouth, and at the same time to impress us, by word of mouth, with their poverty?'

'Aren't you being a little hard on them?' Philip asked. 'Your cousin Charlotte struck me as being quite a sincere person, and as I said, devoted to your interests.'

'My interests, perhaps,' said Giles bitterly. 'There was a time when she was devoted to me, not to my interests, which indeed were nil. I've no idea how much money they have—it looks as if they have a lot, in spite of what you say—but would they, after all these years of silence and neglect, have asked me to stay with them if it hadn't been for the threat to their prosperity of Grandad's second Will?'

Usually inarticulate, except in making noises encouraging or discouraging to his sheep, Giles drew breath, exhausted by the effort to make known to his friend the feelings he had long tried to conceal from himself.

It took Philip just as long to answer.

'I can't advise you,' he said, 'even if you asked me to. One thing I'm sure of—Charlotte is still as attached to you as she ever was.'

'Let's have another drink,' said Giles. 'We can't have this on the moors, can we?' And while it was coming he said, 'I don't want to have anything more to do with her. I shall have to see her again, of course, but I shall make that quite plain. She is Marcus's pigeon, not mine. We shall be off tomorrow, thank goodness, leaving our sting in our tails. I shall be leaving my sting, that is. You have been too kind, Phil, in helping me through this nasty time with my rather nasty relations. Hurrah for Cumberland and the sheep!'

There was a moment's silence, and then Philip said:

'I promised your cousin I would have a drink with her here this evening. We are all dining with your aunt and uncle, of course.'

Giles gasped. Recovering himself he said, 'I don't know what proposition she will make to you. But please, please, Phil, make her understand that I am not prepared to give way one iota on Grandad's Will.'

'I'll tell her,' he said, 'but I dare say she won't bring the matter up. She'll talk about you, though.'

'Let her,' said Giles. 'I'm not interested.'

'I never thought of you as a vindictive character,' said Philip.

Giles scented, and slightly resented, the implied criticism in this.

'Nor did I,' he said, 'and I don't think I was, but that may have been because I had nothing to be vindictive with. Aunt Judith and Uncle Seymour had most of Grandad's money; Charlotte married for money, no doubt thinking she would inherit their money as well. You see how they live, in spite of their protestations of poverty. How could my mother and father and I be vindictive effectually, when we had only a few sheep between us and bankruptcy—*failure*, as it's sometimes called, such a good word—until you, Phil, came along and put us out of the red, or nearly. Did any of them care whether we sank or swam? Not a bit. But now, when they see the red light, they ask us to stay—at least they ask me to stay—you must be a surprise for them, but a very welcome one—hoping to work on my good feelings about the Will—which may cost them £50,000—but they won't succeed.'

'In working on your feelings?'

'No, or in the law-courts either, from what my solicitor tells me. They'll have to stump up.'

'Your Aunt Judith or your cousin?'

'Between them they'll have to find the money, unless they've spent it, which I don't suppose they have.'

Revenge, revenge! Giles's placid pastoral countenance looked quite different under the influence of this new emotion, so long dormant, now activated for the first time.

Philip sighed.

'I quite see how you feel, but I would like to remind you of one thing, though it may not weigh with you. I'm sure that Charlotte is still in love with you.'

'Let her be, let her be!' said Giles, as he had said before. 'If she had shown her love in a different fashion, things would be different now.'

*

At dinner Marcus made them six—he had managed to escape from his important work at Bristol, as Judith explained before he arrived, to be present at this very special occasion. Giles, as before, sat between his aunt and Charlotte. Philip sat on Charlotte's left; then came her father, their host, and then Marcus, whom Giles had seen before but hardly recognized. He looked tired, as Aunt Judith said he was; his clothes, obviously expensive, didn't indicate poverty, but perhaps he lived in a world where good clothes were essential, *pour se faire valoir*.

He didn't talk much, the wine flowed, the silver shone, but the conversation didn't; it flagged, under the constraint of a subject which was in everybody's thought but couldn't come to their lips. There were two exceptions. Aunt Judith, with her social expertise, never let the talk die down, and although Giles found Charlotte's remarks, and the looks she gave him, increasingly difficult to answer in kind, or even very kindly, conversation with some meaning and freedom in it every now and then spurted up between Charlotte and Philip, her neighbour on the other side.

But Giles was, and knew himself to be, from the deferential glances cast in his direction, the hero of the hour, the lost sheep returning to the fold, the pride of the flock, full of honour though not yet of years. He held them in the hollow of his hand; but it wasn't a comfortable feeling, and the new Giles, with all his power, wasn't on good terms with the old one, who had so little.

CHAPTER XXVI

BEFORE they started the next morning on their long trek northwards, Giles had a telephone call.

'It's Phil here.'

'Good morning, Phil. I hope you're none the worse for last night.'

'Oh no, I enjoyed it very much.'

'That's more than I did.'

'I'm sorry, but what I meant to say was, would you mind if we took off a little later, say about 11.30? The reason is, I have an assignation with your cousin Charlotte, if the bar is open by then, or even if it isn't, and I'm sure she would like to say good-bye to you.'

'I said good-bye to her last night, Phil, but I wouldn't mind saying good-bye to her again, in fact I should quite like to.'

'Well then, could you pick me up at the Royal about 11.30? That would get us back in time for dinner, wouldn't it? It took us about eight hours to come.'

'Certainly,' said Giles, trying to stifle the rasp in his voice. 'Do you want us to take Charlotte too?'

'No,' said Philip, laughing. 'But I dare say she would come.'

*

Giles duly arrived at the appointed hour but the hotel porter told him that parking was particularly difficult that morning; could he take a message?

'Yes,' said Giles, nothing loath. 'Please tell Mr. Oakeshott, who is probably in the bar, that Mr. Holroyd is here.'

In a minute or two Philip appeared, suitcase in hand, followed at a discreet distance by Charlotte.

'Hullo, Giles!'

'Hullo, Phil!'

'Hullo, Charlotte!'

'Hullo, Giles!'

These salutations over, Giles said with a new note of authority in his voice, the fifty-thousand pound note, it might be called, 'I think we ought to be off. Good-bye, Charlotte, and thank you. I shall be writing to your mother and father,' and without more ado, he started the car up, and left her standing at the kerb.

What a pretty place Havant used to be! And how pretty it still was, the old town with its inlet to the sea, and yachtsmen, appropriately clad, meeting on the pavements and saluting each other, without a care in the world! And the smell of the sea, coming up intensified through the estuary, as through a funnel! As such smells will, and as such sights will, they brought back to Giles poignant memories of his childhood, when he and Charlotte used to trickle along these streets, every turn of which brought back some old sensation, looking in shop-windows, vainly coveting what they saw, and snuffing, as if it was an elixir, the mingled smell of sea and land!

But soon they were out where the new town began, the new town of ribbon-development, houses and shops, which proclaimed the modern world and had nothing to do with the Havant he remembered.

No doubt it had something which the old Havant had not, but he disliked it none the less.

'You're very quiet,' said Philip. 'Do say something.'

Giles tried to think of something to say.

'Well,' he said, 'it was good of you to come all this way—and to go back all this way.' He accelerated to overtake a lorry. 'It can't have been much fun for you. It wasn't for me.'

'I could see that,' said Philip, 'but you're wrong as regards me. I enjoyed seeing the set-up, as far as I did see it.

I enjoyed meeting your relations, especially your cousin Charlotte.'

'Why?'

'Because she seemed unhappy, unhappy with that dull husband of hers.'

'She needn't have married him,' said Giles again putting his foot on the accelerator. 'She sold her birthright for a mess of pottage.'

Old memories of Bible-reading seemed to unite him to his former self.

'I suppose you could call Marcus a mess of pottage.'

'Well, you said yourself he isn't very exciting.'

'Perhaps she doesn't want to be excited,' said Giles irritably. 'She used to, that's all I can say.'

Were he and Philip on the verge of a quarrel?

'I dare say she didn't know her own mind,' said Philip.

'Oh, she told you that?'

'Yes, it cropped up somehow. And her mother is a very formidable woman, so unlike yours.'

'Well, what do you propose I should do? The decision doesn't lie with me, the money was left to Mother.'

'Couldn't you persuade your mother to make some provision for your aunt and—and for Charlotte?'

'I dare say I could,' said Giles, unwillingly. 'Mother is very kind-hearted, but I don't see why I should. Aunt Judith has had the benefit of the money all these years, and she was quite well off when she got it—at least Uncle Seymour was. I don't mind betting that between them they still have pots of money. Look at the style they live in—we are paupers compared to them.'

Philip said nothing.

'Besides,' went on Giles, warming up, 'the legacy from Grandad's second Will may have to pay a second lot of death duties— we don't know yet what the legal position is—and there may not be much left of the £50,000 when the Government and the lawyers have had their whack.'

Philip considered this.

'I wouldn't dream of advising you, Giles, still less of preaching to you, but I wonder if you wouldn't have been happier if I had never found that Will in the fifth volume of Gibbon's *Decline and Fall*.'

'You may be right, Phil, but I'm damned glad you did. Now we shall be able to get a proper car, instead of this bloody old rattle-trap, which can't even overtake a pram. If it hadn't been for your kindness in leaving us your car, which is a sight better than this one, Daddy would have had to walk. It made me quite sick to see Judith's Bentley and Charlotte's Mercedes, and all the time them pretending how wretchedly poor they were. It's been my aunt's theme song from the beginning,' he added bitterly, 'and now Charlotte has taken it up. I may be a Shylock, but I mean to get every penny that the law allows me.'

'And what does your mother think? After all, your grandfather's second Will left the money to her, as you say.'

'Poor darling, she doesn't know what to think, but she will when we get home and tell her about the flesh-pots in Havant.'

'And what will your father say?'

'Oh, Daddy, he's so engrossed in his work, he's so sheep-minded, he doesn't seem to take in the difference Grandad's Will will make to us. He's made a pattern of his life, founded on resignation. And he works himself to the bone, but he'll keep the money; he'd be a fool if he didn't.'

'And you, Giles? What difference will it make to you?'

'Well, you can imagine, can't you? No more financial worries, no more appealing to the Bank for an overdraft, which, with this financial squeeze, they can't, or won't, give one! You don't know anything about that, Phil, money-wise you're independent. Thank God for that, and thank you, for otherwise where should we be? It sounds a bit selfish, but you know what I mean. And besides—'

'Yes?'

Giles hesitated for a long time. His eyes were fixed on the oncoming traffic.

The Will and the Way

'And besides, I should like to get married.'

Philip availed himself of the privilege of their old friendship. 'Have you anyone in view?'

'No, but I have something to offer besides myself.' He smiled. 'Someone might come along.'

Philip glanced at his companion, at the profile, weather-worn and yet delicate, and felt sure that someone might come along.

'Soon we must stop and have lunch,' he said. 'Lunch will be on me, remember. Something quite strong. But I shall be very abstemious, so I'll drive.'

They drove on in silence until they came to somewhere northwest of Reading which looked like a lunchable town.

'I think of your cousin, Charlotte,' said Philip suddenly. 'You know, she still adores you.'

'How do you know?' asked Giles, in the challenging voice, with an accent of hostility in it, that was new to Philip.

'Because she told me.'

Giles remembered once more Charlotte's letter, written at the time of her marriage to Marcus, and it seemed to him then, even more than it had at the time, not the *cri de coeur* that it really was, but as something distasteful and even disgusting.

'I dare say you're right,' he said, 'but she doesn't mean anything to me now.'

'She would leave Marcus in a moment,' Philip said, 'if you lifted a finger.'

'I wouldn't have her as a gift,' said Giles, taking his hands off the wheel.

'You have lost all interest in her?' asked Philip in a neutral voice.

'Yes indeed. Anyone can have her for all I care.'

CHAPTER XXVII

SOON after dinner Philip retired to bed, pleading fatigue. He had shared the driving with Giles, but he hadn't Giles's whip-cord frame. But tiredness was not only his excuse for going to bed early; he wanted to be alone with his thoughts and he suspected that the Holroyds would want to be alone with theirs. So, with the volume of Gibbon under his arm, he made his excuses and withdrew.

*

'Well, Giles,' said his father—who himself was looking rather tired, healthily tired, for fatigue brought out his inner resistance, just as on most people it has the reverse effect—'How did it go, at Havant?'

His mother, who was darning a pullover, looked across at her son anxiously. 'I wondered how Philip would get on. They were all strangers to him.'

'Well, actually I think he got on better than I did,' said Giles. 'I couldn't help feeling annoyed at the luxury in which they lived—the champagne and so on—and Philip naturally enjoyed it.'

'How did he get on with Charlotte?'

'Oh, like a house on fire.' There was a touch of resentment in Giles's voice.

'And Marcus?'

'Marcus only put in an appearance the second evening. He'd been in Bristol on business. He looked a bit pale and withered—you know, lines under his eyes and some flesh growing under his chin, dewlaps we should call it—as men do who lead a city life. Not much colour in his face.'

'And Judith?'

'Oh, Aunt Judith was the same as ever. Apologized for answering the door herself, because the maid was out.'

His mother smiled.

'That's Judith all over. But I expect she had everything under control?'

'Yes, she had, except for an hour or two when Charlotte had a drink with Phil at his hotel. I don't know how much she liked that.'

'So he stayed at an hotel?'

'Aunt Judith said she couldn't put him up, there was no room in the house. It's pretty big—she might have stretched a point. But she was like she always was, very well dressed and complaining of poverty.'

'What did they say about the Will?' his father asked. 'They know all about it, our solicitors have written to them.'

'They didn't mention it, except indirectly, to say how hard up they were. Phil felt quite sorry for them, especially for Charlotte. They made a great fuss of me, however. I might have been their long-lost son.'

'Well, I'm glad you have come back to us; I never quite understood why you went.'

Unlike many young men, Giles didn't resent his father's criticisms, direct or implied.

'It was partly curiosity, to find out how the land lay. And then it was an outing. We don't have many outings, do we?'

'It's God truth, we don't,' Jack said.

Hester, sitting between them, seeing how like they were to each other, that elegant spare stature, those high cheek-bones, watersheds from which the pale skin, sunburn-proof, flowed like a river, wondered which of them she loved the best. But there was a furrow on Giles's brow that wasn't on his father's.

'Well,' went on Giles, 'I wanted to see the set-up—it's eight or nine years since I was in Havant—and I wanted to know how they would react to Grandad's second Will.'

'But did you find out?' his father asked with a smile.

'Not in so many words. But of course they didn't know that Phil was coming with me.'

'Did Philip coming make any difference?' his mother asked.

'I think it did. They might have opened out to me more if he hadn't been there. Charlotte may have opened out to him'—and again the furrow creased his brow—'but I don't know and I don't much care.'

'Did you think she was tired of Marcus?' his mother asked. 'It was you she really cared for.'

Again the furrow.

'I've no idea,' said Giles, as if such niceties of human relationships meant very little to him. 'But I got the idea that they were all frightened, though they wouldn't show it.'

'Frightened of what?'

'Frightened of Grandad's second Will, and what it might cost them.'

A silence fell between the three.

'I'm not too happy about it myself,' said Hester. 'Of course it would be nice to have the money, but we've got on without it quite well, haven't we?'

'We shall get on better with it,' said Jack, 'and I expect Giles thinks the same.'

Giles nodded vigorously.

'It will mean a lot of unpleasantness,' said Hester, 'supposing we get it, supposing we get it. I know that my dear sister is a designing, intriguing woman. But she is my sister, and I don't like the idea of their whole way of life, which is founded on money, being upset, whereas ours—' She stopped.

'Whereas ours?' queried her husband.

'Well, it hasn't depended on money. We haven't had enough to depend on it. I dare say that in some ways—quite important ways —we are better off than they are. Happier, for instance.'

'How? Why?' Jack asked.

'Well, we have our little place, our niche, in the countryside, we don't owe anything to anyone—thanks, I admit, to Phil—'

'We shall still have Phil, all Phil and heaven too. Besides, the law must take its course. Grandad wanted us to have the money, for reasons you know quite well, and they don't reflect much credit on your sister, as you yourself admitted, and his last wishes should be respected, even if they are in your favour. Are you suggesting that we—'

'I'm not suggesting anything,' said Hester. 'I only hope it will turn out all right. I sometimes suspect windfalls.'

'We've never had one,' said her husband, 'except when I married you,' and he leaned across and kissed her. 'We'll try and make the best of it—if we get it. What do you think, Giles?'

'I'm all in favour,' Giles said. 'Does mother think we ought to hand it back to them? For bigger parties and more champagne? I think we could put the money to better uses than they could.'

'But supposing they haven't got it?' Hester asked.

'Well, they'll have to stump up what they have got.'

His mother sighed.

'You seem to have taken against them, Giles. You never used to be like that.'

'Well, I am now,' he said. 'I shouldn't mind seeing them bankrupt.'

CHAPTER XXVIII

THE case of Holroyd v. Snape dragged on and on. It was quite certain what the upshot would be, so Jack's solicitors told him; but every objection was made by the Snapes'. Had old Mr. Handforth been in his right mind when he made the second Will? After all, he had had one stroke. Yes, he was in his right mind. His doctor, who was still alive, had testified that Mr. Handforth had been perfectly *compos mentis* when he, Mr. Handforth, signed the Will. But was it not possible that someone had brought undue influence on the ageing, if not actually mentally infirm Mr. Handforth to change the terms of his Will? To which the Holroyds' solicitors had their answer ready. Who did they mean by someone? Well, anyone. By anyone, did they mean other relations of Mr. Handforth? But he had no other relations, except his younger daughter, who lived in distant Cumberland and who only saw him two or three times a year, whereas his elder daughter, Judith Snape, who lived on the spot— But Mrs. Snape had devoted her life to him. If he even had a headache, she was at hand —was it likely that her father would have made this cruel Will, depriving her of everything, unless—? Here Mr. Handforth's old friend James Mackenzie was called, and very reluctantly said how he had told Mr. Handforth, because he felt it his duty, that Mrs. Snape was not on the bread-line, as she pretended to be, but was expecting a large sum of money from a merger which her husband was arranging. But did he get this large sum of money? Mr. Snape, forty-eight and rather shabbily dressed, said it was true about the merger, but that it was of much less value to him than

The Will and the Way

rumour made out, as he could easily prove. He had told his wife about it, who was on the verge of a nervous breakdown thanks to their financial embarrassments, and to one or two business friends, who he hoped would have more confidence in him.

'And their confidence has been justified in Mr. Snape? But I don't understand why Mr. Handforth's second Will should have been kept secret all this time. Was it an act of vindictiveness on his part, was it a time-bomb which, as some old people do, he hoped would explode after his death? Surely, if he had been as vindictive as that towards Mrs. Snape, his daughter and his benefactress, he would have made his second Will known, so that he could have relished her discomfiture in comfort—?'

'He wouldn't have had long to relish it, as he died two days later—'

'Yes, but he couldn't have foreseen that. He might have kept it up his sleeve as an unpleasant surprise, supposing she did something that he didn't like. It's known as "Will-shaking," I believe, a practice some elderly people have, a kind of blackmail to keep their heirs, or potential heirs, in a proper state of subjection—but why should Mr. Handforth have wanted to keep his beloved daughter, to whom he owed so much, in what you call a proper state of subjection?'

This was the weak point in the argument of the solicitors who were acting for the Holroyds. However, they knew the reason why Mr. Handforth had made a new Will: his friend, to whom he had confided his disgust with Judith's behaviour, had disclosed it—and the law must take its course.

Judith, when called on to give evidence, said with great dignity she could think of no possible reason why her father should have made a new Will.

And so the verbal wrangle went on and on. It was fully reported in the local newspaper at Havant; it was fully reported in the local newspaper in Cumberland; it even got a mention in the London press. Hester and Jack suffered misery from it but Giles, who knew what the inevitable outcome would be, followed the proceedings with great interest.

'It looks as if we are sure to win,' he said to his mother.

'Yes, darling, I hope we shall, but what a bother it all is.'

'Aunt Judith and Seymour will have to pay the costs, you know, if they lose, and we shall be on velvet.'

And to Philip.

'What do you think about it, Phil? As for me, I'm glad to think they're going to be reckoned up. Aunt Judith is a real bitch, and as for Uncle Seymour, I'd rather not say what I think about him.'

Philip looked uneasy.

'I rather wish it hadn't happened. Or I wish it hadn't happened through me. So much unpleasantness—I keep being asked about it. But you don't mind?'

'Not a bit, so long as we win.'

'You don't mind about Charlotte, who was once in love with you—and what will happen to the rest of them if they are all ruined?'

'I don't, and I'm quite sure they won't be. Aunt Judith has cried poverty every day of her life, and did she mind if we were left more or less penniless—I mean penniless compared with her? No, it will do them good if they have to reduce a little their standard of living—one bottle of champagne less.'

*

'Dear Charlotte,

As I said in my last letter, I couldn't be more sorry for what you are going through now. Your Aunt Hester and your Uncle don't enjoy it—the publicity I mean—but what must it be like for you, who are in no way responsible for your grandfather's second Will? I only wish I had never found it! Giles doesn't seem to mind the publicity—he's a changed man, and just thinks of what he is going to get if he and his parents (who are much less keen on it than he is) win this law-suit, as I dare say they will. Giles works on as usual—he is as strong as a horse—but he doesn't talk as much as he used to, and I know his mind is fixed on the money he hopes to get from your mother's estate. It's very sad. Even if I could sympathize with him, he's not the companion he used to be—always with this on his mind—though I can't blame him in a way, for everyone here that we know talks about it, as I dare say they do, though not so much, where you are.

What a miserable state of affairs! I hope it will soon be decided one way or the other, unless, as I fear, the verdict, if it goes against your mother, will be a serious blow to you financially.

As I said before, I enjoyed the time I spent at Havant very much. It was such a change from the rather Spartan life we have here. I oughtn't to say that, for your aunt and uncle are kindness itself, and so is Giles, or he would be if he could rid his mind of this obsession about the money. It's so odd, he never seemed to give it a thought until I found the Will. I suppose it triggered off a grievance he's had for many years, but suppressed as long as he knew there was nothing he could do about it.

You told me you were fond of him, and I'm sure he is still fond of you, but he wants his pound of flesh, or rather he wants it for his mother. At least that's my impression. He doesn't say much about it—he doesn't say much about anything—but I can almost feel it working at the back of his mind.

I'm sorry you're not altogether happy with Marcus; I don't really know him, of course, but I can see he's not much of an emotional stand-by.

I wish you could visit us here, but it's not for me to invite you, and I'm not sure you would be comfortable in our very different way of living, sharing a bath-room and a loo with the rest of us, and very simple meals at odd hours, when we come in from farm work and when your Aunt Hester has time to cook them.

But in any case, with things as they are between the two families, you probably wouldn't like to come.

You kindly asked about my health, and I'm glad to say that both the doctor and I think it's much better for my sojourn here

—I have quite a good appetite, as you may have noticed, though that was partly due to the exquisite *cuisine* at Havant.

I haven't much other news, but I should be very glad to hear yours.

Affectionately,
Philip.

P.S. Apologies for this over-long letter, but I felt constrained to write.'

*

Three days later he had a reply from Charlotte.

'My dear Phil,

I hope you don't mind me calling you Phil (it seems rather familiar but that's the way I think of you). It was a joy to get your letter, and I only wish it had been twice as long. You are right—this wretched business about Grandpa's Will has been, and is being, a great worry to us. It's plain that the poor old fellow was in his dotage when he made it, but legally it seems to be quite in order, and if the case goes against us, as I'm afraid it will—will, will, will, the word is a recurrent refrain in my mind—it may be awkward for us, for mother at any rate, for it is she who will have to fork out the money, if she can, poor dear, though Marcus no doubt will be called in to help. And I suppose that if we lose we shall have to pay the costs as well. I think it was a mistake that we ever decided to fight it. I can't see Mother destitute, can you? But it may come to that.

I did hope that Giles would see reason, and make some sort of compromise. Who would have thought he could be so revengeful? We were great friends once. I dare say he resented my marriage to Marcus; but he was in no state financially to marry, at least Mother thought so and no doubt she was right.

Que faire? Marcus doesn't tell me what effect the loss of the money will have on us; Mother will have nothing—poor Mother, for poor she will be, who was always so good to Grandad—she almost devoted her life to him, she danced attendance on him, even if he had a cold in the head—I can't imagine why he made this Will.

Marcus hasn't told me much about it—I suppose that husbands never tell their wives much about their financial affairs, and Marcus has never been very communicative about anything. Heigh-ho! But it was, and is, a great relief, dear Phil, to have your sympathy in these times of stress.

If you can face the journey again, with or without Giles, I should be overjoyed to see you—Marcus may be in Bristol, but we should all of us love to see you, if Aunt Hester and Uncle Jack and Giles can spare you. I do envy you your peaceful and prosperous life in Cumberland!

With my love (if I may),
Charlotte.'

CHAPTER XXIX

THE case of Grandad Handforth's Will dragged on, but after some months it was settled. The result had long been a foregone conclusion. Aunt Judith lost, and had in addition to pay the costs of the action, which were considerable. How she reacted to the verdict was not known to her sister, for by then relationships between the two families were quite broken off. There were still some legal difficulties to be dealt with. Was Grandad Handforth's second Will liable to Death Duty? The Inland Revenue typically said it was; but the Holroyds' solicitor argued that the estate had already paid death duty once, it need not pay it a second time.

This was finally agreed to; and the local newspaper (no doubt in touch with the local paper in Havant) came out with the headline:

THE HOLROYDS WIN!
£50,000 FOR AGRICULTURE IN CUMBERLAND!

And there were many favourable comments on this in the pubs round about, for though neither Jack nor his son frequented them, they were known to be hard workers, and paid well for casual labour when they needed it and could afford it. Besides, it was a victory for the North over the South—an ancient rivalry—a victory for people who really *worked*, in the snow and the rain, come bad weather or worse weather, over the Southerners, who basked by the sea, with little on themselves or to show for themselves.

Giles couldn't but be pleased by this popular acclaim; he had never courted it, so it was all the more gratifying for being publicly demonstrated. When opening time came, he drove to the nearest hotel and bought two bottles of champagne.

He didn't conceal the happiness in his face—he felt twice the man he was—and the landlord didn't conceal his.

'Why, Mr. Holroyd, we must congratulate you on your splendid success! It's a triumph for you and for all of us! You must have a drink on the house, and may it be followed by many others! Now what would you like?'

Giles, who was not used to drinking, elected a gin and tonic, and while it was coming he looked round shyly and a little nervously at the company in the bar, some of whom he knew by sight and a few by name. They all smiled at him, and when his drink arrived they raised their glasses.

'Good luck to you, Mr. Holroyd!'

Giles, who was not really accustomed to bar etiquette, and still less to popular applause, raised and glass and said, 'Here's to you!' Their smiles rewarded him, and he suddenly had an idea.

'Can we have drinks all round?'

'Of course,' the landlord said, but while he was asking the others what they wanted, in a sudden panic he fumbled in his pocket—supposing he hadn't enough to pay? He was so used to the idea of not having enough money to pay for this or that—but happily the wallet which Charlotte had once given him contained the wherewithal, not only for the champagne, but for the well-wishers around him.

It is not good manners, in such circles, to turn your back on the bar, and this Giles knew; but having remembered to ask the landlord to join him, he turned round and rather sheepishly said, 'Good health!'

'Good health!' they all replied, with as much evident pleasure in his success as if it had been their own.

*

Riches, riches, how wonderful they were after what now seemed to Giles, slightly befuddled as he was, years of privation! To be able to go into a bar of one of the smartest local hotels and buy two bottles of champagne! And to pay for a round of drinks for the other patrons of the bar, and not one round, but two. He wished it had been three, but as he got into the car, the family car, and felt his head, unused to alcohol, giving slight signals of vertigo, he was glad he hadn't.

Giles returned to Helvellyn Farm, with the two bottles of champagne under his arm, more excited than he had ever felt before. He didn't realize that his life had been a series of frustrations; he only felt the enormous relief from them that Sisyphus might have felt if unburdened of his load. And more than that, he felt the heady brew, the intoxication of popular acclaim which he had never had before, and least of all during the past months, when chilly waves of unspoken, unwritten resentment had rolled up from Havant, down the English Channel, up the Irish sea, and landed somewhere not far away on the coast of Cumberland.

He wouldn't have dared to buy the champagne or the rounds of drinks but for his visit to the Bank that morning. He had always crept almost surreptitiously into the Bank, whether to pay money in or to take it out; and the request he had made more than once for an overdraft had been woundingly refused. So near was he to the red, if not actually in it, that he had a besetting fear that his cheque might 'bounce', in spite of the fact that his father, who had lived for so long in the district, had a small but regular account there. But he didn't want to be financially dependent on his father, or rather on his father's good name.

This morning when he went into the Bank, after the news of the Holroyds' coming fortune, confirmed by the law court, had been splashed about in the newspaper, how different had been his reception! The cashiers, male and female, stared at him from behind their counters, as if they suddenly realized what a finelooking man he was; and when he timidly asked the manager if he could have an overdraft of £50, the manager replied, 'Of course, Mr. Holroyd, a hundred if you like.'

Such thoughts, such warm, comforting thoughts, accompanied him on his way home.

It's a poor heart that never rejoices, and when he reached home

The Will and the Way

and saw the table that his mother had laid for dinner, with the familiar jug of water in the middle, he plonked down the two bottles of champagne and said, a little tipsily:

'Fizz!'

'Fizz?' echoed his father, eyeing the bottles as if they were something that might explode (as indeed they later almost did, for neither he nor Giles had the technique of opening them).

'Yes, fizz,' repeated Giles, impenitently. 'You've seen the paper, haven't you? I thought we ought to celebrate.'

'A very good idea, my boy,' his father said, 'a very good idea.' He glanced at his wife, who was on her way from the kitchen. 'Giles has bought us some champagne. Don't you think it's a good idea?'

She stopped and regarded the festive bottles, their necks encased in gold foil, their corks bulging with challenge to a *sommellier*. 'I expect it is a good idea, just for this once. What do you think, Phil?'

Philip, who had been hovering round the table with the critical expression of an expert examining a still-life, said, 'It's O.K. by me.'

'Then who shall we drink to?' giving the champagne a sidelong look.

'To ourselves, of course,' said Giles, still 'under the influence' of his welcome at the bar. 'Who else is there to drink to?'

No one answered this, and when the corks had at last been extracted by eager but unpractised hands, and had rebounded with a glorious report from the ceiling, they drank to each other.

CHAPTER XXX

AFTER the verdict confirming the validity of Grandad Handforth's second Will, a stillness, almost a hush, descended upon the Holroyds, as if they were sailors who for most of their lives had been battling with angry waters and had suddenly come into the calm. They hardly knew each other or themselves, so great was the change. They didn't talk much about it, partly because each member of the family had a different reaction to it, and was diffident of exposing it to the others—all except Giles, who openly rejoiced. He ordered himself two new suits, he began to take a pride in his appearance, which well deserved it, he returned quite often to the bar where he had scored his initial social success. He felt himself to be *someone*—not an anomalous being, half-way between a labourer and a small farmer—who needn't kow-tow to anybody, or have to assert himself in local society.

With Jack, his father, the impact of the Will was different. He had never felt a grievance and so didn't feel the relief from it that his son did. For many years he had lived in straitened circumstances and was used to them and resigned to them. He was what he was; a farmer among other farmers, less successful than most no doubt, but with his place which he maintained by the sweat of his brow. If he couldn't always pay up at once, he owed no one anything for long and regarded himself, without rancour, as a poor relation of the human family, of whom there were many poorer than he. The idea that he would now be in a privileged position and able to look down on his neighbours, through no effort of his own, bemused him, and when they met him and

The Will and the Way

congratulated him on his good fortune, as they often did, he felt in a false position, elevated by something that had happened outside and beyond his own efforts, and was apt to apologize.

With Hester it was different again. She seldom mentioned their change of state. She, the lucky one, the recipient of this windfall, thought of it in terms of her own family. Why had her father suddenly changed his mind? What did it all mean? She knew that her sister was a scheming, designing woman but, as someone said, anything could be forgiven between sisters; and the thought of their childhood together and their mutual affection, when Judith's bossiness did not offend her gentle compliant spirit, though it often indeed rather strengthened it to face situations which she could not have faced alone—the family, headed by Judith, against the world!—all this came back to her, and she did not rejoice as she might have done at Judith's downfall.

Philip kept his feelings to himself, though he thought about his future, and wondered how Charlotte would face this long drawn-out but not unexpected blow.

*

The money, of course, was not immediately forthcoming; a great many forms and documents had to be filled in, and witness-signed before Grandad Handforth's bequest could be transferred from Judith to her sister. The interval was a sort of financial no-man's-land, of which the end was always in sight but always receding. Giles, impatient, used to ring up the solicitors every other day and ask when, if ever, his mother was going to get the money. But while the Holroyds were still being subject to the law's delays and to hope deferred which (in Giles's case) maketh the heart sink, an event occurred which could not but effect, if it did not essentially alter, the whole aspect of the situation. It was announced by a letter, shortly followed by two others, all bearing the Havant post-mark:

'Dearest Hester,
  You will no doubt have seen in the papers the sad news (Hester

hadn't seen it) that Marcus has died. His health, as you know (Hester didn't know) was never very good—he worked too hard; and when he heard that the case of this extraordinary Will of Grandpa's had been settled in your favour, he had a stroke and died soon afterwards.

The funeral is tomorrow. I thought that perhaps some of you would have come, but I expect you are too busy.

Seymour and I are aghast at this dreadful happening. Marcus and Charlotte were *devoted* to each other. They hardly spent a day apart since they were married. They depended on each other *absolutely*. It was a true union of souls—so rare in these days. Since Marcus's death I have spent most of the time I could spare from household chores with Charlotte, trying to comfort her. She is bearing up bravely, poor girl, but *what* she must be going through!

We have always been so close to each other, dearest Hester, that I feel I can mention another matter, the matter of *money*, as indeed it was directly responsible for Marcus's death. He always wanted to give her the best he could—and who can blame him? I don't know what their financial position is now—as you can imagine, it must be at a pretty low ebb, or Marcus wouldn't have spent so much of his time in Bristol, which he hated. I don't know what will happen to her now, poor girl, or what will happen to her two children. I suppose she will have to sell their house, which without spending much on it she had made so pretty—and then what? What about her children's education? A poor widow, how can she provide for it?

There is another thing. I don't want to speak of it, especially "at this stage" as they say, but I think I must. Seymour and I gave all the money we could spare—it wasn't much—to Charlotte when she married—a "marriage settlement", I believe they call it. It left us rather short, and we have always been trying to do and make do, not very successfully, as you must have noticed the last time you came to stay.

And now Seymour tells me that because of Daddy's Will we

shall be in Queer Street—we may have to sell this house and buy a cottage, if we can afford it—I must say I dread the thought of that.

I needn't tell you how I envy your position up North, with flocks of fat sheep around you and no money worries, for everyone knows that farming, if it isn't the quickest way of making money, is the slowest way of losing it.

Blood is thicker than water and so I appeal to you, dearest Hester, to make some provision for us out of the fortune that Daddy unexpectedly left you.

Your ever loving sister,
Judith.'

The second letter was much shorter, and was addressed to Giles:

'Dearest Giles,

You will have heard our sad news, but I won't say anything about it now, for I am only just beginning to get over the shock.

Marcus was the dearest of men, always with me—he was hardly ever away from home, except for the first of the two nights you stayed with us, and then he rushed back from Bristol so that he could see you.

I am so miserable now, and so are the children, who can't yet realize what has happened ("But where's Daddy?") nor, luckily for them, what is likely to happen. It is all too sad, and sometimes when I'm not too upset by thinking of the present, and what the future may or may not bring, I think of our happy times together, as children, when we were almost in love with each other, weren't we? But it's no use thinking of the shining past when the present is so dark.

Do write to me.

With all my love,
Charlotte.'

Giles only answered this letter with a rather formal letter of condolence. He wasn't a great letter-writer, and Charlotte, he felt, had passed out of his life. But he didn't and couldn't ignore the undertone of feeling in her letter; it brought back a feeling, a sweetness of feeling, that he had never known since, and which had turned sour when she married Marcus.

The third letter was also from Charlotte—it came a week later, when she was beginning to get over her grief:

'My dear Phil,

It was so sweet of you to write and condole with me, and console me. I can't tell you how much I appreciated it but also the kind thought behind it, which seemed to shine through every word, warming as well as shining. You are indeed a good friend.

It has been, as you say, a dreadful time—Marcus was the best of men and the kindest of husbands (the only one I've ever had!) and though we didn't always see eye to eye on some things (food, for instance) we were always happy, together or apart. He was rather wrapped up in his business, in which (between ourselves) he wasn't as successful as he was thought to be, but he always had time to make room for me, and fit me into his life. Heigh-ho! His death is not only a great shock and a great grief, but it seems to have taken the ground from under my feet; not only emotionally, but in many other ways—I hardly know where I am, or where to turn next, for I don't think I can afford to stay here. Perhaps I can find a little house not too far from Mummy and Daddy, or I could live with them, if they have room for me. But I rather think that they, like me, may have to sell *their* house in order to raise the money, and in any case, fond as we are of each other, they are so accustomed to their own way of living, that they might not like to have their widowed daughter and her two children foisted on to them. Ralph and Angela are little darlings and give no trouble, and I'm said to be a good cook, and could help them out on the domestic side if they have to part, as I expect they will, with their old standby, who has been with them since I was a baby.

It is all very difficult, especially as I haven't yet been able to find out yet what our financial position really is. Marcus was a good businessman, but he liked entertaining and lived up to his income, I fancy, and may have had other commitments outside his household expenses. I believe he had made some provision for the education of Ralph and Angela, but I simply don't know. Men are so cagey about their business affairs and Marcus, much as I loved him, was no exception.

What do you think? What do you advise? Your letter was so kind and sympathetic and so *understanding* that I don't feel ashamed of asking you what you think I ought to do.

Yours affectionately,
Charlotte.'

Philip kept her letter in his pocket and took it out and brooded over it from time to time. He also conveyed some of its contents, as much as he thought it would be discreet to disclose, to the older Holroyds; but he didn't mention it to Giles.

CHAPTER XXXI

MEANWHILE Hester and Jack held a council of war—or, as Hester wanted to make it, a council of peace.

'I do feel rather uncomfortable,' she said when they were alone together, 'about the situation my sister and Charlotte find themselves in. I know, as you do, Jack, that Judith is designing and mercenary and perhaps not over-scrupulous, but at the same time she is my sister, and Charlotte is my niece, and I don't like the thought of their living in penury, just because Daddy changed his Will.'

'We know why he changed it, at at least we have a shrewd idea.'

'Yes, but his friend James Mackenzie, to whom he confided his reason for making this second Will, was a notorious gossip, and I shouldn't trust too much to what he said.'

'Your father thought it good reason enough for changing his Will,' said Jack flatly.

'Yes, darling, but had he? To himself, no doubt, he had; but was he quite himself when he made it?—he had had one stroke when he made it, and died almost immediately afterwards of another. And why did he *hide* this second Will?'

'Because, I suppose,' said Jack, 'he shrank from the unpleasantness of letting Judith and Seymour, and other people, know about it. He probably meant to take it from its hiding place when he knew he was dying and would be too far gone to mind what anybody said, but he didn't have time.'

Hester's face was still troubled.

The Will and the Way

'Well, we know about this famous merger, and how Judith is supposed to have concealed it from him—but we must remember that she had done a great deal for him, even if her motives were a little—what shall I say—*smelly*, to use a nasty word. But the fact remains that she was his stand-by, while I was living happily here with you, and couldn't have done much for him even if I had wanted to.'

'I didn't know your Dad very well,' said Jack obstinately, 'but he was a good man, and good to me, and I don't believe he would have changed his Will without a good reason.'

Hester shrugged her shoulders.

'I'm not so sure,' she said doubtfully. 'And if it's true what Judith says, and what Charlotte says—'

'How do you know what Charlotte says? Has she written to you?'

'No, only to thank me for my letter of sympathy.'

'Then how—?'

'She wrote to Phil, apparently, and said the same thing—that Daddy's mind was affected at the end of his life.'

'Why did she write to Phil?'

'I've no idea. I suppose he wrote to her, and told her he felt sorry for her.'

'I didn't know they were on those terms,' said Jack rather sharply.

'Nor did I, but they must have met when he and Giles went to Havant for that party. Does it matter?'

'No, it's just a surprise. Marcus wasn't ill then, was he? I suppose that he and Charlotte met after that.'

'Very likely.'

'And then she wrote to him? It seems a bit sudden.'

'Did you write to Charlotte about Marcus?'

'As a matter of fact, I didn't, I knew you were writing to her, and I thought that would do for us both. I'm not mad about Charlotte. She's had quite a good time, in one way and another.

'What do you mean exactly?'

'She's had her fun, and so has he, in Bristol and other places.'

Hester realized that for the first time in their married lives they were on the verge of a quarrel.

'I don't think we need go into that,' she said. 'The point for *me* is'—and she emphasized the word *me*—'what are we doing to *do*? Are we going to let them go down the drain, sell up and lose all their standards of comfort, or are we going to help them?'

'My dear,' said Jack, 'it's for you to decide. Your father left his money to you, not me.'

Hester knitted her brows and said what she had been preparing herself to say: 'Should we divide the money with them?'

Jack turned away. 'As you like, my dear. It's for you to decide.'

Hester's distress was now obvious, and her likeness to her sister who for one reason or another always wore a troubled brow, was more obvious, too.

'We've been very happy together, haven't we?'

'What, you and me?'

'Yes, who else?' And at the unexpected harshness in his voice, her face puckered.

'We've been happy together, without this money from Daddy's Will?'

He shrugged his shoulders.

'We might be happier with it. I'm strong, but I'm getting on in years, and it would be a relief to have something to fall back on, as your sister and'—he hesitated for a moment, as though unwilling to pronounce her name—'and her daughter have always had.'

'They won't have much now,' said Hester.

'But how do we know that?' asked Jack fiercely. 'Are you sure, Hester, that they aren't pulling the wool over your eyes? They were supposed to be almost millionaires once; do you think they can be so broke now that fifty thousand pounds would make the same difference to them as it would to us? I know their tricks and their manners,' he said, with a sudden memory of Dickens that only the emotion of the moment would have recalled, 'and I

The Will and the Way

should like to see their bank-accounts before you give away a penny of your father's money.'

His wife looked at him with incredulity and horror.

'Do you mean that they are *lying*?'

'They have lied before,' said Jack.

The conversation stopped.

Jack got up and walked round the room.

'There's one thing you seem to have forgotten,' he said, 'in your anxiety for your family's fortunes.'

Hester was near to tears now.

'Giles. We haven't much to give him, except what we get from Phil, and precious little to leave him. He's a good boy—he works hard—and I think you should consider him, even if you don't consider me, before you hand the money back to your family.'

The tears were now coming into Hester's eyes. She wiped them away, and said:

'Isn't it really a question of *happiness*? We've been happy all the years we've been together, haven't we, living on a pittance, I know, but with enough for our needs, for mine, at any rate? It won't make any difference to our way of life if I give the money to them—we shall carry on as we always have but they—'

'Yes?'

'Well, my sister will have to sell her house and Charlotte, apparently, will have to sell hers.'

'What makes you think that Charlotte will have to sell hers?'

'Philip thought so. She said something about it in her letter to him.'

'Phil seems to know a good deal about Charlotte's affairs. How do you account for that?'

'Oh, because she wrote to him and he told me the gist of it.'

'Your family is a very mercenary family,' said Jack, with more severity in his voice than Hester had ever heard him use, 'and it wouldn't surprise me if—' He broke off.

'What, dear Jack?'

'Just this, dear Hester. You are of course at liberty to give away the money if you want to; but if you give it to your sister and her daughter, you will obviously be going against the testator's wishes. I don't know if it weighs with you or not, but he obviously left the money to you in order *not* to leave it to them, when he heard about the merger—'

'Yes, I know about the merger.'

'He knew that Judith and Seymour were far better off than they let on. When he realized she had been working on his feelings and making out that she was much worse off than she was—he changed his feelings. We won't go into it again. But I wish I could find out how much money Judith and Charlotte actually *have*. I don't mind betting they still have plenty of money, far more than we shall ever have, even with your Dad's legacy.'

Between her tears, and made almost inaudible by her tears, Hester said:

'I can't believe you. You never liked my family. Is there no way of finding out how much money they have?'

'I don't think so. It's the sort of thing that Banks don't reveal.'

Hester dried her eyes again.

'I think you're being rather mean, Jack. Whatever Daddy's motives may have been when he made his second Will, it will make far more difference to them than it will to us. It will mean a fall in their standard of living, which affects people more than anything these days, and it won't make any difference to ours.'

'Not even to our standard of loving?' asked Jack, in whom the strain of the conversation had brought out a long-latent wit.

'No, why should it?' asked Hester, pursuing the course of her one-track mind. 'We shan't suffer; they will. I can't understand why you don't see it.'

'How do you know we shan't suffer?' Jack asked.

'But how can we? We shall go on as we used to.'

'One never knows what may happen,' said Jack, anxious to bring the controversy to an end. 'But before you decide to give

The Will and the Way

the money back to your family, I do think you should ask Giles, unless you feel he has nothing to do with it.'

'I will, of course,' said Hester, and for the first time she spoke with the authority of someone who is in secure possession of a fortune, 'but I'm sure he will see reason.'

CHAPTER XXXII

GILES came in late for lunch, or dinner as they preferred to call it, apologized and sat down.

'Of course it doesn't matter,' his mother said. 'But where is Phil?'

'He's gone away,' Giles said. 'That's partly why I was late. He went away early this morning.'

'By car or by train?'

'By car—his car, I needn't say.'

'Where to, if I may ask?'

'To Havant, I think.'

There was a minute's silence at the table while Jack munched his food; Giles attacked his, but Hester left hers untouched.

'Why did he go to Havant?' she asked.

'He didn't tell me; I've no idea, unless he was going to see how Charlotte was getting on.'

'Oh, Charlotte,' said his father, looking up between mouthfuls of mutton. 'Then they are chums, are they?'

'I suppose so,' said Giles, in what was for him rather an acid tone, 'or he wouldn't have gone. He wouldn't have gone just to see Havant—besides, he's been there before.'

'I expect he's sorry for Charlotte,' said his mother. 'We should have gone, Jack, shouldn't we? We *ought* to have gone. But it was all so unexpected. Phil will tell us about it when he comes back. How long is he going to be away?'

'A day or two, I think.'

'I wonder he didn't tell us he was going.'

The Will and the Way

'He did tell me,' said Giles, hungrily, 'but I hadn't time to tell you, because I had to dash out and do his work as well as mine.'

'It's very unlike him,' said Hester.

'People don't always act like themselves,' said Jack, tolerantly. 'Perhaps he'll tell us when he comes back.'

*

Hester took the opportunity of Philip's absence to discuss with Giles the problem of her father's Will.

'Daddy,' she said (she still sometimes referred to Jack as 'Daddy', as she had when Giles was a child), 'thinks we ought to keep the lot. I don't. I've heard directly from Judith that she and Seymour may have to sell their house and live in what is called reduced circumstances—and I've heard indirectly, through Phil, that Charlotte will have to do the same—if together they are to raise this £50,000.

'I've been through all this with your father, and he thinks we should stick to the £50,000 which the court has allowed us (and they had to pay the costs of the case, which must have been considerable). It will mean a heavy drop in their standard of comfort, which is what people of today dread more than anything.'

'Well, ours couldn't fall much lower.'

'Oh, Giles, how can you say so? You make me feel you have never been happy with us. It's true we have an outside loo, but we have an inner bathroom, which is more than many people have. And we're so healthy! Look at me (I own I'm not much to look at), but look at yourself, if you want to see a picture of healthfulness! *You* won't die of a heart-attack just because you've heard some bad news.'

'You never know,' said Giles.

'No, but I don't think so, because you've never led the self-indulgent life they lead in Havant. But it's different for them—they will have to give up all sorts of luxuries, and even necessities, that they are used to, but which we're not. It's an old saying, but it's a true one, that you don't miss what you've never had. I'm not defending them, I'm just saying that health-wise, and in my case happiness-wise, we can better afford to do without the money than they can.'

'Then what do you propose?' asked Giles gloomily, after a pregnant pause.

'I propose,' said his mother, 'and I think Daddy can be brought to agree with me, and I hope that you will agree, that we shall divide the money—£15,000 to Judith, £10,000 to Charlotte and the other half to us, £10,000 to Daddy and me, and £15,000 to you, which will be a help, won't it? We shall have Phil's contribution, which had tided us over the difficult time, and we shall all be that much better off.'

Giles was silent. The elation of the moment when he had learned of the Court's decision and bought the champagne, to the congratulations of his fellow-company in the bar, seemed to fall flat. He knew it was unreasonable: £15,000 was a tidy sum (he had hoped it would be much more), and yet he grudged it to his aunt and his cousin, who had turned down his suit (or rather *her* suit, for it was she who had made the running, backed up by her mother) and left him high and dry on the fells, with no ability or even inclination to reconstitute his life on other lines—on the lines which the £50,000, his family's inheritance, would have traced out. 'I'm sure you're right,' he said, in a voice that implied she was wrong. 'Let's go on as we were.'

His mother, family-bound, who had felt so sure of her case, suddenly felt a twinge of doubt and even of compunction.

'I hope you're happy about this?' she said anxiously. 'I quite see that if we had *all* Grandad's money, we could give up farming and live somewhere else—I don't quite know where, Bournemouth, perhaps where so many retired people go to live and,' (she smiled) 'to die, and perhaps you would like that better.'

'I'm not sure I should,' said Giles gruffly, trying to sort out his mixed feelings.

'I know it's dull for you here, but Phil is a companion for you, isn't he?'

The Will and the Way

'Oh yes, he is,' said Giles, trying to reconcile the reality of the known past with the promise of the unknown future. 'Phil is a good chap and I'm fond of him.'

His mother's face relaxed; her whole body seemed to relax; and the chair she sat in seemed to relax too.

She drew a long breath, only half aware of the emotional strain she had been through, talking to Giles.

'When he comes back, when Phil comes back, you must ask him what he thinks. I'm only your mother, and I don't want to bring pressure on you,' and she got up rather shakily and kissed him.

CHAPTER XXXIII

'Hullo, Giles!'

'Hullo, Rosamund.'

'It's such ages since we met.'

'Just wait a minute,' Giles said. Helvellyn Farm was a small house, and the telephone was in the hall, within hearing-range of anyone who happened to be passing, and after checking that the coast was clear, or appeared to be clear, Giles rushed back to the telephone.

'I'm so sorry, Rosamund,' he gasped. 'I didn't know if there was anyone about.'

'Would it have mattered if there had been?'

'Of course not. What were you going to say?'

'Only just, hullo, and to ask how you were all getting on.'

Giles racked his brains for what he should, and should not say, and said,

'Well, we've had a sort of law-suit.'

'Yes, so I read in the local rag. And I'm very glad you won it. It will make a difference to you, won't it?'

Caution, caution.

'Yes, it will, though not perhaps as much as we thought.'

'I'm sorry to hear that, I hoped it would make you all millionaires.'

'Oh no, far from it.'

'Forgive me for asking, but does it affect Phil in any way?'

Giles took a hasty look round the hall, and the two doors, three including the staircase, still in darkness, which led off it.

The Will and the Way

'No, Phil has his own money.'

A moment later he regretted saying this.

'Is Phil still with you?'

'Yes, but he's not here at the moment.' Anything to uncomplicate matters.

'Where is he?'

How full of curiosity women were.

'Well, as a matter of fact, he's in Havant, visiting my mother's relations. He'll be back quite soon.'

'When he comes, remember me to him, will you? And perhaps you and I could meet in the meanwhile? I've almost forgotten what you look like, but I should know you if I saw you.'

'Yes, let's,' said Giles, suddenly aware of his hunger for female companionship, and remembering also, with a sense of personal afflatus, the £15,000.

'Could we make a date?'

'Yes, any time next week. At the Troutbeck, for instance? That's a half-way house between us, and the food is quite good, I'm told. Shall I ask Phil to come too?'

'Well, not unless you want to.'

Before the kitchen door opened, they had arranged a date.

*

When Philip returned they all were naturally anxious to hear the latest news from Havant.

But Philip was not very communicative and a little evasive.

'How did you find Judith?' her sister asked.

'Not very well. Her son-in-law's death has been a great shock to her, of course.'

'I can understand. It has been a great shock to all of us.'

'And she doesn't know which way to turn. Seymour was quite beside himself.'

'I know, he's devoted to her. But was there anything else?'

Philip hesitated.

'Yes, there was the question of the money they have to raise for your father's Will. They don't know how to find it. But you will know about that.'

Jack and Hester exchanged glances.

'Did you think they were hard up?' Jack asked.

'They didn't exactly say so, but they intimated it, and their general situation had obviously gone down. No sign of a housemaid, no drinks, except a little vin rosé at mealtimes.'

'You couldn't have had much fun,' said Giles, sipping his cider.

Philip was also sipping his.

'Oh, I don't know, but I was sorry to see how their—their standard of life had changed.'

There was a slight pause, and then Hester said:

'And Charlotte—how did you find her?'

A number of expressions crossed Philip's face.

'Poor Charlotte, she was in a rather dreadful state, you can imagine why. She had been married to Marcus, how long? Eight or nine years at least. You would know. And they had hardly ever been separated—'

'Excuse me, but I rather doubt that,' said Jack. 'There were all those visits to Bristol.'

'I know; Charlotte spoke of them, for they were a terrible *corvée* to him, as they were to her. She said they undermined his health—sleeping in hotels and so on, wherever he could get in—and then the news of your father's Will finished him off.'

'Did she talk much about money?' Jack asked.

'Well, not more than she could help,' answered Philip, a little indignant. 'You couldn't expect her to, could you, in the circumstances? It wouldn't have been, it wouldn't have been—you know what I mean. But she did say she was pretty hard up, because they had always lived up to their income, and sometimes more, and she didn't know which way to turn after the bombshell of her grandfather's Will.'

'Did you gather,' asked Jack in a voice quite unlike him, 'which way she meant to turn?'

The Will and the Way

'She didn't say,' said Philip, shortly, 'and I couldn't ask her. She sent you all her love and good wishes, and said how much she would like to come up and see you all, but circumstances made it impossible.'

Supper was over; Philip, who was tired from his journey, and Giles, who was tired from extra sheep-tending, retired to bed. Hester and Jack were left alone.

'We must do something for them,' Hester said. 'It would be too selfish to keep all Daddy's money for ourselves. You did agree, didn't you, Jack, that we should divide it—half to them, £10,000 to us and £15,000 to Giles? That's not unreasonable, is it?'

'Not to you, at any rate.'

CHAPTER XXXIV

FORTUNES, if they come at all, come singly; misfortunes, as we know, come in battalions.

In the case of the Holroyds it wasn't battalions, only a small squad, but active enough to be upsetting.

Judith, with the help of Charlotte, had paid up the £50,000 from old Mr. Handforth's second Will. They had lost the lawsuit, and furthermore they were unable to prove to the satisfaction of the Holroyds' solicitors that they had spent the money and therefore couldn't pay up. A cheque was received for the amount from Judith's solicitors.

Her sister spent the day in tears; Jack tried, but not successfully, to conceal his jubilation; he put the cheque, in its envelope, in the pocket of his workaday jacket, and on a rather cold day it literally kept him warm. Every now and then he took it out of his pocket to make sure it really existed.

He did not come home, as Giles had on the report of the cheque's imminence, with two bottles of champagne; but he came back looking years younger, and too obsessed with success to notice that his wife looked ten years older.

The next step, which he punctually observed without having to be reminded of it by Hester, was to send Judith a cheque for the other half, £25,000. He asked her if she would rather do this, but she only shook her head.

Jack's pleasure in his good fortune was not damped by this, nor by having, as promised, to part with half the fortune. Nor was it lessened, but rather increased when, with Hester's permission, acknowledged with a nod, he wrote out a cheque for £15,000 to Giles and, finding a moment when the two of them were alone (a conjunction rare at Helvellyn Farm), he handed him the cheque and actually kissed him, a demonstration he hadn't made since Giles was a lad. Giles, embarrassed but warmed by pleasure, that brought out his latent affection for his father, returned his salute; it was quite a touching scene.

Later, Philip, who was still studying Gibbon in his bedroom, joined them for supper; and the meal, in spite of Hester's red eyes and long bouts of silence, passed without mishap, such is the emotional elation that money gives.

Almost immediately the Holroyds began to make improvements, or to order improvements, at Helvellyn Farm. Indoor sanitation was the first; new carpets, new curtains followed, and Hester was quite enough of a housewife not to enjoy these changes which she had always secretly longed for.

And the house must be repainted and redecorated inside and out: this was her province, and the choice was left to her, though she was careful to consult Philip as to what curtains he would like in his room, and what wallpaper.

Soon the house presented an entirely new appearance, and the Holroyds, refreshed by the change from shabbiness to smartness, felt themselves twice the people that they had been.

*

The work of restoration, renovation and redecoration went on uninterruptedly, and as far as the male members of the household were concerned, uninterruptingly, for they were out-of-doors before the workmen came in and not indoors before they went out. It was for Hester to bear the noise and the bustle and the dirt they left behind them. She supplied them with all the newspapers she had, old and new, to obliterate the marks of their tramping feet; and they in their turn made as little mess as they could help. A kind of friendship grew up between them and her; they did not resent her suggestions, nor did she resent theirs; they knew the latest thing in house-decoration, whereas she, who had been nearly thirty years at Helvellyn Farm without changing anything that hadn't dropped to pieces, was not. She began to take a keen interest in these renewals and to feel herself renewed by them, as by new shoes, a new dress, a new hat—luxuries of which she had long deprived herself. Rather timidly she began to indulge in them and felt she was entering into the world of fashion, that mysterious, over-alluring world, which most women find irresistible, even if they have not the means to make it theirs.

It was slightly disappointing that when Jack and Giles and Philip came home, sheep-worn and tired, they did not always notice the progress that had been made during the day, and had to have it brought to their notice, but even they partook, consciously or not, of the afflatus of the general renascence of Helvellyn Farm.

CHAPTER XXXV

THE friendship between Giles and Rosamond prospered, and after a time they were seeing each other whenever Giles could find release from his duties on the farm, which turned out, as is often the case with affairs of the heart, to be more often than his strict timetable allowed. All the same, he didn't feel quite happy about it, for hadn't Rosamond once shown a partiality for Philip, who was a much better match than he was, even with the extra £15,000? Philip worked for his health, Giles worked for his living; Philip's health contributed to the Holroyds' wealth, but it wasn't quite the same thing.

One day when Giles and Philip, accompanied by an over-officious sheep-dog, were pursuing an errant sheep to its proper destination, Giles said to Philip:

'You know, Phil, how things are between Rosamond and me?'

'Well, I had a shrewd idea.'

'And you don't mind? I thought at one time you had a fancy for her yourself.'

'I had, but I haven't now. She's a nice girl; go ahead, Giles, and good luck to you.'

At this moment the dog's over-industrious efforts at the heels of the wanderer from the fold needed a reprimand.

'ROVER! ROVER!'

Rover returned with a slightly shamefaced but self-righteous expression, as of one who had only been doing what it was his duty to do.

'Good dog, good dog,' said Giles, patting the apologetic Rover, who now cowered behind them. 'We aren't engaged yet. But since we've had this money from my grandfather—can you believe it, it's actually been *paid*—I am in a position to . . . to . . .'

'To offer her your hand?'

'Yes, you can put it like that.'

'ROVER!'

The dog, who had become impatient at being denied his sheep-folding instincts, returned, crestfallen, to heel.

'It's a shame,' said Giles. 'He could do this job better than we can, but he over-excites them and does them no good. What I was going to say, Phil, was that if we got engaged, and afterwards got married, it won't make any difference between you and me, will it? We shall probably try to find a little place of our own nearby and you could live with us, if you wanted to, or with Daddy and Mummy—they'd be only too glad to keep you. So should I and Rosamond be—she's always had a soft spot for you.'

'ROVER!'

The dog came back, wagging his tail and showing signs of penitence.

Giles patted him and muttered words of encouragement and discouragement. 'I wouldn't like to be a dog,' he said, 'at everybody's beck and call. Not that Rover is; he wouldn't pay the same attention to other people that he pays to you and me. But what I meant to say was, you're in favour of me and Rosamond getting married?'

'Of course I am,' said Philip. 'In any case, it's for you to decide.'

Giles shook his head. 'I've been a bachelor for a long time, as you have, Phil—it will need a good deal of . . . of readjustment. I suppose I'm set in my ways. I put marriage out of my life, because I couldn't afford it—not in any way that would make it worth while—until now. It's different for you, you're independent, you can marry when you want to, but I hope you won't.'

'ROVER!'

'I never knew such a dedicated animal,' said Giles crossly, as

The Will and the Way

Rover returned with what could only be called a sheepish expression. 'No, I'm not pleased with you,' he said, refusing his hand to Rover's offered head. 'You mean well, but you're making a nuisance of yourself.'

Rover crouched behind them until the lost sheep had been safely gathered into the fold.

*

Not long after Jack and Giles had agreed to the equal distribution of Mr. Handforth's Will between Judith's family and theirs, there appeared the announcement in the papers that Marcus had left £135,000—death duty so much.

'We can't do anything about it,' said Jack. 'She's got her whack from us, too. Like mother, like daughter. I warned you, Hester, I warned you.'

Consternation reigned.

'Of course,' said Hester, defensively, 'it doesn't mean that Judith has been left well off. She told us that she and Seymour had given all they could afford to Charlotte, which no doubt accounts for what seems to us this large sum. She may still be badly off.'

'In that case,' said Jack, 'I hope Charlotte will help her out, as we have.' He didn't try to disguise the bitterness in his voice.

'Charlotte has her children to think of,' said Hester, seemingly unperturbed. 'They are young, and education is so expensive nowadays. Happily for us, Giles is educated and settled in life.'

'Yes, but do you know, Hester, that he wants to get married, and if he gets married, he may have children to educate?'

'You mean Rosamond?' said Hester. 'I've never known how serious he was about her, or she about him for that matter. She had quite a *tendresse* for Phil at one time. In any case, that's all in the future; he has his niche here, and I for one should be sorry to lose him to a girl I don't care much about.'

'That's his concern,' said Jack. 'I don't think it should influence us.'

He was clearly very angry.

'Your family has always meant so much to you,' he went on, 'and you think they can do no wrong.' He saw the tears brimming in his wife's eyes, but they didn't deter him.

'Giles has been a very good boy, worth a dozen of your worthless family, and I think you should consider him for a change.'

Hester's tears burst out.

'Haven't I slaved for you and him, Jack, all my life, when I might have, when I might have—' She couldn't think, still less say, what she might have done while Jack was waiting for her to speak—but at length a thought crystallized in her mind. Upset though she was, she knew instinctively that it would be too wounding to him, and too dangerous to her own happiness, to put into words. She knew that a deep affection built up over the years can be destroyed for ever by a single word. But she had to say something to justify herself and relieve her pent-up feelings, so she found a substitute for that which might have broken up their marriage.

'I needn't have married for love.'

Angry as he was, Jack took the point, and said what had been in her mind to say:

'Yes, you could have married a man for his money, as your niece Charlotte did.' The effort to get rid of his resentment nearly choked him, but struggling with his emotions began to prevail over it.

He jumped up from his chair and walked to and fro, unwittingly displaying those aspects of himself, unaffected, perhaps even accentuated by age and hard work, which Hester had always loved and admired. Sitting down again he said haltingly, and aware that in this day and age the phrase was almost ludicrously old-fashioned:

'You have been a very good wife to me, Hester. After all, the money is yours and yours to dispose of. I know how much your family has always meant to you, and if you wanted to give them the whole of it—'

The Will and the Way

'I don't,' said Hester, staunching her tears. 'I only wanted to help them, to keep them from penury. We don't rely on money, as they do, we rely on something else.'

Convinced, indeed flattered, by her argument and now rather ashamed of himself, Jack nodded.

'O.K., darling, O.K.,' he said, thankful, as many men of his kind are, to bring a painful situation to an end.

CHAPTER XXXVI

THE course of true love never did run smooth, still less the course of love that is not so true. Giles hadn't been in a position to marry and he hadn't realized, when he had been a cross between a shepherd and a sheep-dog and perhaps not so useful as the latter, how much he wanted to be married or, if not married, able to indulge the mounting sexual cravings natural to a man of his age. Hard work, as is the case with many manual workers, who go to bed too tired to think of anything but sleep (or sheep in his case), had kept such cravings at bay; now, with the possibility of having a legal and unimpeded outlet for them, to which nobody could object (for he was sensitive to his parents' and to public opinion, besides having the labouring man's semi-indifference to sex), he began to want it. And, as a friend had told him, when you are married you can have it whenever you want it.

He wasn't in love with Rosamond; nor, as he realized and as she realized, was she in love with him; but they had both known each other for a long time and they both wanted to get married. When Giles had received Philip's assurance that he was no longer interested in Rosamond, he began to take the matter more seriously. He didn't want to find out whether other girls in the district might be more to his taste or he to theirs. He supposed, and was right in supposing, that many a girl whom he had seen in the distance, and been slightly attracted by, would have once regarded him as financially ineligible—'something better than his dog, a little dearer than his horse'—had he possessed a horse. He didn't even possess a car—he borrowed his father's, or used Philip's, whenever they were available.

Giles's mother had married beneath her both socially and money-wise. She and his father had lived on her marriage settlement (until her father's death), on his untiring efforts as a farmer and of course latterly on Philip's contribution of money and work. Giles, without being a snob, didn't want to marry beneath him; and now he needn't, for the £15,000, with his own efforts as a sheep-farmer, would put him in much the same social and money bracket as Rosamond was.

Equality was perhaps as important as love, even if love was the stronger incentive. As it was, he didn't clinch matters with Rosamond, as he would have if he had really been in love with her; he took it for granted there was an understanding between them; she came more frequently to Helvellyn Farm and was welcomed, though not exactly with open arms, by his mother and father, and by Philip, her one-time lover, who now looked at her abstractedly and a little askance.

Rosamond played up as well as she could against—not hostility, for there was none—but a certain lack of overt enthusiasm, which extended even to Giles. Whereas when he visited her parents' house—though he sometimes hesitated on the threshold —he was sure of a warm welcome. He was now of course a much more frequent visitor than he used to be; in fact, before his grandfather's legacy he had seldom been in their house; it was much more spruce than his mother's and father's. Rosamond's parents too were farmers, but on a bigger scale than his. They regarded their one child Rosamond as something very precious— 'keep off, keep off!' they had seemed to say to young men who were interested in her—but now that she was twenty-eight, the same age as Giles, they began to feel she ought to be settled in life, and when the news of Giles's windfall was spread abroad they felt so all the more.

Meanwhile, Giles busied himself with ways and means. What small house or cottage could he buy for them both, and for the family they would have? For he, accustomed as he was to sheep-rearing, could only think of marriage in terms of a large progeny, and more and more did he feel that he had it in him to create one and that Rosamond was to be the medium of this creative act.

When they were in company together, or when they were alone in each other's company, they didn't have much to say to each other. She waited on his words without contributing many of her own. The future was their province, not the present, the future with their children about them—and Giles was never a great conversationalist, since his conversation with sheep didn't have to be articulate: 'Whoop-ooh! Fetch 'em in, Rover!'

*

'Are you sure you're on the right tack?' Philip asked him.

'The right tack?'

'Yes, with Rosamond.'

If Giles had been in love with her he might have taken offence.

'I don't see why not.'

'Well, have you much in common with her?'

'We both want to get married,' said Giles, 'and have a family. I'm tired of a single life. Isn't that enough?'

'I'm not sure it is,' said Philip.

'I'm not sure it is,' he repeated. 'You and I can talk about things that interest both of us, but I get the impression that you and she don't have much to talk about. Life stretches ahead—I'm only asking.'

'Well, I don't ask for much,' said Giles, 'only to get out of the rut I'm in. I'm tired of my routine—'

'I know what you mean. But couldn't you find something more exciting than bed and breakfast, and working the rest of the day?'

'Could you, Phil?'

'Yes, I think so. I had a slight feeling myself for Rosamond once, but she's a dull girl really, in spite of her romantic name. Can you think of yourselves together of an evening, with not a word to say, and infants screaming overhead?'

'It's better than quarrelling,' said Giles.

'I dare say,' said Philip. 'But it seems to me a bit of a bind, you

The Will and the Way

an intelligent man, sinking into a pit of domesticity with only a few sheep to help you out.'

'Can you think of anyone better for me?' Giles asked. 'Charlotte, for instance?'

'No, not her, not her, on any account. But some girl with her head above water, who would sympathize with you and argue with you and disagree with you—and take you out of yourself and make life more interesting for you.'

'Show me one, Phil. I'm not engaged to Rosamond.'

'I'll keep my eyes open.'

But he didn't.

CHAPTER XXXVII

THE next event was not only a surprise but a shock.

'May I talk to you for a moment?' said Philip to Jack in the no-man's-hours, the hour of relaxation, for the men of the household at any rate, while the evening meal was being prepared. It was for them an hour of dispersal, each of the three feeling free to pursue his own thoughts and his own activities, or inactivities. Giles, as Philip knew, was paying one of his evening visits to Rosamond, not many miles away. Fragrant kitchen-smells were penetrating the sitting-room. Jacked seemed to be in brown study—or was he half asleep, weary of the long day's toil?

At any rate he didn't answer.

'May I have a word with you?' Philip said.

'Of course, my dear fellow,' said Jack, coming to himself with a start. 'I seem to have been in a sort of day-dream. What was it you were going to say?'

'Only this,' said Philip, who had already prepared what he was going to say, and knew it almost by heart. 'I'm engaged to be married.'

Jack sat up from his recumbency, and the day-dream, if it was one, vanished. He tried to attune his thoughts, and his words, to greet this bomb-shell, but all he could think to say was, and he put into it all the enthusiasm he could:

'I congratulate you. And may I ask who is the lucky woman?'

'It's your niece Charlotte.'

Jack sat bolt upright.

'Charlotte?' he said. 'Charlotte? Charlotte?' and at every

repetition of the name his voice changed. 'And I'm afraid that means you will be leaving us?'

'I'm afraid it does, sir,' said Philip, who had never called his employer-employee 'sir' before. 'I'm afraid it does.'

'I didn't think you knew Charlotte,' mused Jack, 'well enough, well enough to—'

'I've only seen her a few times,' Philip said, 'and that was when Marcus was still alive, though he was away at the time. And I've seen her once since. We seemed to get on well together. But I don't want you to think—I don't want you to think—'

'Yes?' said Jack, who was thinking of many other things.

'I don't want you to think that Marcus's Will had anything to do with it. We were—we were attached to each other before I knew about his Will, and engaged too, but Charlotte didn't want it known; it was too soon, she thought, after Marcus's death. She wasn't very happy with him,' he added, spreading out his hands, 'those visits to Bristol, and so on—well, I don't know. But I felt sorry for her, and pity can lead to love, as it did in my case.'

Jack didn't know how or where to look, so he got up, as his habit was in times of emotional stress, and took a few paces to and fro.

'My dear boy,' he said at length, 'I can only wish you joy. Charlotte is a clever woman and a clever manager, like her mother.' He hesitated for a moment and then let the question which was underneath his thoughts rise to his lips. 'What will your present and future plans be, if I may ask? Will you go on farming in these regions, as I hope, or will you betake yourself elsewhere?'

Philip lit a cigarette, an unusual indulgence for him.

'I think,' he said, 'that Charlotte would like me to move down into her part of the world. There must be openings there—if not in farming itself, then something to do with farming—which I might hope to get, thanks to my experience with you.'

'I'm sure you're right,' said Jack. 'There must be farming near Havant, as there is elsewhere. Not sheep-farming, I should guess, but agriculture of some sort. Charlotte, I believe, is very adaptable—she may make an ideal farmer's wife.'

Philip, on whom the disclosure had been a greater strain than he cared to show, got up and said, 'Perhaps you would be kind enough to tell Giles about this when he comes in. He's such a good companion—Rosamond is a lucky girl.'

In confusion, he hastily left the room.

*

'I don't know when would be the best time to tell Giles,' Jack said when he and Hester were together in their ample, iron-clad matrimonial bed, still sleepless after midnight.

'I'd rather you did, Jack. Give him a drink or two—whisky, perhaps, we've got some drinks in the house now. But do you think the position is as bad as all that?'

'It's not worse than it was, it's just the same as it was,' said Jack, who had said this more than once before. 'Phil was been paying us £15 a week for his board and lodgings and tuition—if you can call it so—and then there was the work he puts in—he's always worked hard—he must be worth at least £20 a week to us, besides using his own car.'

'And now?'

'Well, now, instead of being paid, we shall have to pay someone else. We shall be back in square one—or square minus one.'

'Couldn't we find another apprentice?'

'You remember what trouble we had in finding Phil. He was a godsend. And now that we've spent so much money on the house—relying, as we did, on Phil still being with us—we shall be in the red again.

'What shall we do?' asked Hester, turning her head uneasily on the pillow, and not finding in her husband's sturdy body the comfort and response that she used to.

'We shall have to ask Giles. He's better off than we are.'

*

Giles was appalled by the news. It knocked him sideways. How could he now go on with his matrimonial plans, leaving his mother and father deeply in debt, worse off, thanks to their outlay on the improvements at Helvellyn Farm, which were still going on, than they had ever been?

Philip was still with them, but for how long? Advertisements for a new apprentice received no replies; advertisements for another farmworker received replies, but the wages they asked for seemed exorbitant.

At meal-times silence reigned. Jack could not forgive Hester for parting with half her patrimony; Giles could not forgive her either, nor could he quite forgive Philip for ploughing with his heifer, when he made this clandestine arrangement with the still-married Charlotte, possibly ignorant of her affluence.

None of them made any approach to Judith; even Hester did not reply to her letter saying she was so delighted to hear that poor bereaved Charlotte had come to some kind of understanding with Philip, whom she had always liked so much; 'he's a dear boy', she said.

Giles was the one to suffer most. True, he still had his £15,000; he was under no obligation to contribute to the renovation of Helvellyn Farm; he could just go ahead with Rosamond. He was, if not exactly engaged, deeply and publicly involved with her. He could not withdraw from their relationship without loss of face, loss of face to him, loss of face to her, and both being made a laughing-stock.

If he had loved her more, and his parents less, he might have gone through with it. As it was, after weeks of self-interrogation, an experience with which he was unfamiliar and which was all the more painful, he decided he couldn't.

'Rosamond,' he said one evening, as he was driving her back from his home to hers in the car he had lately and proudly bought, 'there's something I ought to tell you. I don't want to, but I ought to.'

'What is it, darling?' asked Rosamond sleepily, for since Grandad Handforth's second Will on special occasions they had wine for supper.

'It's this,' said Giles, and he had never felt so miserable in his life. 'You know that Phil is leaving us?'

'You said something about it, but how does it affect you and me?'

Giles didn't know the saying 'Never apologize, never explain' and felt he should do both.

'It's like this,' he began. 'Phil is leaving us, like I said, and he's going to marry Charlotte.'

'Yes, you told me,' said Rosamond, still unconcerned and still sleepy. 'But what difference does it make?'

'It makes this difference,' said Giles, wondering if he was in control of his new car and could pass the breathalizer test. 'Mum and Dad' (he sometimes used this up-to-date expression, though his mother had told him not to) 'won't be able to carry on without Phil's help. As you know, Rosamond, Mum gave away half the money her father left her in his second Will. Well, they've worked it out, and they find that when Phil goes they'll be worse off than they were before.'

Dimly perceiving the drift of Giles's remarks, Rosamond sat bolt upright.

'But that's their pigeon, isn't it? Your mother needn't have given away the money?'

'No, she needn't,' and Giles sounded as miserable as he felt, and even more resentful. 'She needn't have, but her family has always meant so much to her, and she couldn't bear to think of them in poverty, and though the law was on our side, there was always the doubt, to Mum, whether Grandad was in his right mind when he made that second Will. Rather than leave her sister and her niece on the rocks, as she thought, she divided the money between us and them. That would have been O.K. by us, if Phil hadn't decided to leave us and marry Charlotte.'

'Did he know she was an heiress?'

'He says not. But the net result is that Mum and Dad will be worse off than they were before, and I can't leave them in the lurch.'

'But you can leave me?' said Rosamond.

The Will and the Way

Giles sighed heavily. It was a moment of all moments that he most dreaded.

'We could be married,' he said cautiously, 'if you were prepared to live at Helvellyn Farm with my mother and father. There would be a room for you and me, and an attic room for an apprentice, if we could find one.'

'Where do you sleep?' Rosamond asked.

'In the attic. Phil has the other room—it's big enough for two, and of course,' he added, not to encourage or discourage her too much, 'we now have a loo indoors, as well as a bathroom, though you sometimes have to queue up for it.'

'I thought we were going to have a house on our own.'

'So we were, if this hadn't happened—I mean, if Phil wasn't leaving us to marry Charlotte.'

'Couldn't you find another apprentice?'

'Judging from the difficulty we had in finding Phil, no. A hired man, yes perhaps. But he would want at least £12 a week, and they couldn't afford it. I should have to help them out.'

'Which means you can't get married?'

'Not on the terms I offered to you once. You must forgive me, Rosamond, I couldn't have foreseen any of this.'

They were approaching the short drive up to Rosamond's home. There was a light over the door.

'Is this final?' she asked.

'I hope not,' said Giles, doubtfully. 'Who knows what may happen?'

Nothing happened, at least nothing happened to the advantage of the Holroyds. After a decent interval, Philip and Charlotte were married. The Holroyds were of course invited to the wedding, which took place in Havant; but their excuse for not attending was a true one, they simply couldn't give the time. So they contented themselves by giving Philip, with whom they had no quarrel, and Charlotte, who was not very popular with them but after all was Hester's dear niece, not an ice-box but an electric blanket.

Meanwhile Giles and Rosamond lived in a state of what might be called unarmed neutrality. Each waited, not over-anxiously, for the other's next move. Had they been more in love, they would not have behaved in this half-hearted fashion. But Rosamond felt that lodgings with Giles's parents was not what she was looking for; she might go further and fare better, for Giles, in spite of his undoubted physical attractions—the pale skin and fair hair, in which health and vigour bloomed so unostentatiously —was not the only pebble on the beach. For Giles, with his limited acquaintance in the neighbourhood, there were no pebbles for the moment. Luckily for him, he was attached to the flock, and they gave him a feeling of warmth born of familiarity, and animal sympathy which he couldn't have defined. He could distinguish between each, though to the inexpert, they all looked alike. He had his favourites, and sometimes, when he was counting them into the fold, he would mutter under his breath, 'One, two, three, four—good-night, darling—six, seven, eight.'